FOUR-FOUR-TWO

FOUR-FOUR -TWO

DEAN HUGHES

SCHOLASTIC INC.

FOR MY GRANDSON
JOHN THOMAS "JACK" HUGHES

No part of this publication may be reproduced, stored in a retrieval system, or transmitted in any form or by any means, electronic, mechanical, photocopying, recording, or otherwise, without written permission of the publisher. For information regarding permission, write to Atheneum Books for Young Readers, an imprint of Simon & Schuster Children's Publishing Division, 1230 Avenue of the Americas, New York, NY 10020.

ISBN 978-1-338-18829-5

12 11 10 9 8 7 6 5 4 3 2   17 18 19 20 21 22

Printed in the U.S.A.   40

First Scholastic printing, March 2017

Interior design by Mike Rosamilia, cover design by Russell Gordon
The text for this book is set in Meridien LT Std.

PREFACE

On December 8, 1941, the day after Pearl Harbor was bombed, President Franklin D. Roosevelt declared war on Japan. Almost immediately, Adolf Hitler of Germany declared war on the United States. The three Axis powers— Japan, Germany, and Italy—were now at war with most of the world.

This sudden onset of war was startling to Americans, and many of them panicked, expecting attacks on the mainland of the United States at any moment. Frightened people often imagined their country being infiltrated by collaborators and spies. Immigrant Germans, Italians, and Japanese with ties to their homelands were interrogated and hundreds were jailed. Germans and Italians who had chosen not to become citizens were especially distrusted. The problem for *Issei*— first-generation Japanese immigrants—was that, by law, they were not permitted to become citizens in the first place.

Among most Americans—both private citizens and government officials—suspicion of Japanese Americans was much more intense than suspicion of European immigrants. For one thing, it was Japan that had attacked the United States. But racist attitudes were also part of the culture of the time. General John L. DeWitt, commanding general of the Western Defense Command, recommended to President Roosevelt that all Japanese Americans be removed from the West Coast "war zone" out of "military necessity," and he was later put in charge of the confinement of more than 110,000 Japanese Americans. In his argument for removing the AJA (Americans of Japanese ancestry) from the coast, he stated, "A Jap is a Jap," and explained that statement by saying, "You just can't tell one Jap from another. They all look alike."[1] Later, when an easing of restrictions was being considered, he claimed that the government need not worry about Germans or Italians, "except in a few individual cases," but said that "no Jap should come back to this coast except on a permit from my office. . . . We must worry about the Japanese all the time until he is wiped off the map."[2]

This shortening of "Japanese" to "Jap" may seem

---

1   Asahina, Robert, *Just Americans: How Japanese Americans Won a War at Home and Abroad* (New York: Gotham Books, 2006), *213–14n*.

2   Reeves, Richard, *Infamy: The Shocking Story of the Japanese American Internment in World War II* (New York: Holt and Company, 2015), 160.

inoffensive if you haven't heard the term before, but it carried with it the connotation of all such disrespectful names used for people of various races or nationalities.

Instead of suspected foreign agents of Japanese descent being handled case by case, and only those proven dangerous to America being incarcerated, *all* Japanese Americans were labeled "enemy aliens." (Incidentally, no Japanese American was ever tried and convicted of espionage or sabotage.) Second-generation Japanese immigrants, born in America—known as *Nisei*—were citizens, not "aliens." Most, like Yuki Nakahara, the protagonist of *Four-Four-Two*, had grown up eating fish and rice at home, but also hung out at soda fountains and ate hamburgers and fries with their friends of other races. They danced the jitterbug, wore jeans, and listened to the latest hit songs. They were American kids, but overnight, many of them were rejected and mistreated by their schoolmates.

On February 19, 1942, President Franklin D. Roosevelt signed Executive Order 9066, which directed the removal of enemy aliens from the coastal areas labeled war zones, but the order was only carried out against Japanese Americans. In March, all AJA on the coasts of Washington, Oregon, and California and on the border of southern Arizona were "relocated" to temporary quarters at racetracks and fairgrounds, and then they were moved to camps in remote places around the nation. They were held throughout most of the war in these "internment camps," which were enclosed by barbed-wire fences. Armed guards, in towers, watched their movements.

What was most remarkable about this action was that American citizens were held without any evidence against them or any opportunity to defend themselves in court. They were, in reality, locked up for being Japanese, and very few of their fellow citizens stood up for them or defended their rights.

At the time, 1,300 *Nisei* were members of two National Guard units in Hawaii. It was not legal to remove them from the military, but officials worried that if troops from Japan invaded the Hawaiian Islands, these local soldiers would desert their country and fight for the enemy. The *Nisei* protested and vowed their loyalty to the United States. Nonetheless, government and military leaders decided to segregate them in a separate military unit and ship them to the mainland, at least in part to get them out of Hawaii. They were designated the 100th Infantry Battalion (Separate). The troops in this battalion were entirely Japanese American, but almost all the officers were white.

Once the initial panic in America cooled to some degree and the AJA soldiers proved themselves to be effective in their training exercises, military leaders began to make the case that the 100th Infantry Battalion should be deployed to Europe and enter the battle. Government officials hesitated. Beyond the question of loyalty, some leaders argued that the Japanese soldiers were physically too small to be able fighters.

For most of a year, the 100th was trained and retrained and repeatedly delayed, but eventually the battalion was approved to enter the war in Italy. In addition, another larger military unit of *Nisei* soldiers was created out of volunteers from both Hawaii and the internment camps on the mainland. This organization, named the 442nd Regimental Combat Team, was trained at Camp Shelby, in Mississippi, and was also delayed in being sent to the war. By then, however, the 100th was proving itself not only reliable but even superior to most other units fighting in Europe, and that opened the way for the 442nd to join the action.

What the 100th Infantry Battalion (Separate) accomplished was nearly miraculous. They fought with zeal against the Germans who occupied Italy, and they did so, at least in part, to prove their loyalty. They soon became known as the "Purple Heart Battalion," because so many of them were wounded or killed in action.

Regiments normally have three battalions, but only the Second and Third Battalions of the 442nd were sent to Italy. Not long after arriving, the 100th Battalion was attached to the 442nd and took the place of their First Battalion. Because these troops had made a prestigious name for themselves as a separate unit, the men of the 100th preferred to keep their original designation. As a result, the newly organized unit became the 100th/442nd Regimental Combat Team. Hawaiian Japanese loved to play dice and poker, and a common phrase among them was "Go for broke." This meant "go all in"—bet everything and either win or go broke. It was this phrase that the troops chose as their motto, and so the 100th/442nd became known as the "Go for Broke" regiment.

All this talk of regiments and battalions may be confusing to those who have not had military experience. Let me try to shed a little light on army organization. In this novel, Yukus "Yuki" Nakahara and his friend Shigeo "Shig" Omura are members of a four-man fire team, which is part of an eight-man squad, and their squad is part of a platoon of thirty-plus men. Usually, three infantry platoons make up a company and three companies make up a battalion. Three battalions make up a regiment. Regiments combine to form a division. Divisions form corps, and corps are part of a field army. So a four-man fire team is part of an organization that may include more than eighty thousand soldiers.

The terms for military units most frequently used in this novel are "regiment," "company," "platoon," "squad," and "fire team." The following chart may make it easier to envision those formations. The bolded units are the ones in which Yuki and Shig serve in this novel:

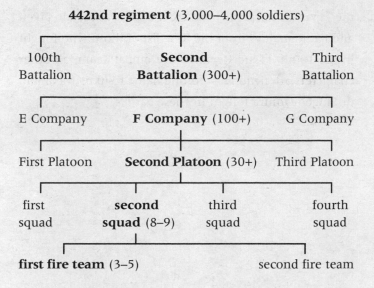

442nd regiment (3,000–4,000 soldiers)

100th Battalion	**Second Battalion** (300+)	Third Battalion
E Company	**F Company** (100+)	G Company
First Platoon	**Second Platoon** (30+)	Third Platoon

first squad · **second squad** (8–9) · third squad · fourth squad

first fire team (3–5) · second fire team

This book is a work of historical fiction. The battles described are the ones that F Company (also called Fox Company) fought, and the locations, names of military units, weather conditions, and dates are all accurate. Details about battle strategy, weapons, actions of individuals, and so on are based on my research, but soldiers' written and verbal accounts vary, and memories sometimes differ; the conversations my characters have, their specific actions, and the feelings they experience, while based on my reading of personal histories, are my creation. Historical figures such as President Franklin D. Roosevelt, Adolf Hitler, and General John E. Dahlquist are included in the book, but, while some of the Japanese names I chose are the same as certain given and family names from the long list of those who fought in the 100th/442nd Regimental Combat Team, all other characters are fictional—no one named Yukus Nakahara or Shigeo Omura fought in these battles.

CHAPTER I

December 1941

Yuki Nakahara was stacking wooden boxes accord-ing to size in a musty storage shed. As he walked past the open door, he saw a car driving up the dirt road toward the farm. It was traveling too fast, jolting, dust billowing up behind it. Yuki stopped and watched. He could see that the car was a new '41 Ford—a fancier car than he usually saw this far away from Berkeley—and Yuki was almost sure he knew what that meant. He felt himself tighten, his chest suddenly rigid, but he had no idea what he should do.

The black car stopped between the storage shed and the house. Two men got out, both of them wearing dark suits and hats. They each turned and looked around, clearly checking out the farm, the buildings. One of the men noticed Yuki, so Yuki stepped from the shed and tried to look calm. He walked toward the tall man on the driver's side. The man removed his hat and asked, "Is your father home, young man?"

Yuki didn't like the look of the guy. His dark hair was combed back slick, and his shirt collar was stiff and bright white—like he was someone official. His voice had sounded polite, but the look in his narrowed eyes was menacing.

"Are you produce buyers, or—"

"We need to talk to your father." The man's tone was suddenly curt, but then he brought it under control as he said, "Would you please take us to him?"

Yuki thought of running to his father, telling him to hide. But he knew he couldn't do that. "I saw him walk into the house a few minutes ago," Yuki said. "I'll see if he's still there." He walked past the man and headed toward the house.

Both men followed, walking fast enough to keep up. The second man—a smaller fellow with a brown suit, black hair, dark eyes—caught up to Yuki at the front door, where Yuki stopped to remove his boots. "Leave your shoes on," the man said. "We'll go in with you. Just tell your father someone wants to see him—nothing else." He had a low, hard voice and some kind of accent, maybe New York. Yuki nodded, but he shoved the door open and stepped hard on the hardwood floor inside. He wanted to make as much noise as possible. The two men separated inside the little living room and stood on either side of him. Yuki thought of shouting to his father, telling him to run out the back door, but Father would never do that. He would be respectful. It was the way he dealt with white people, always.

When Yuki took a step toward the kitchen, the bigger man reached out and grabbed his shoulder, held him back. And then he announced, "Mr. Nakahara, we need to speak to you. We're agents from the Federal Bureau of Investigation."

Yuki's mother stepped into the living room from the kitchen. She was wearing a white apron over her housedress. Her hair was pulled back tight against her head. She was tiny, but now she took a breath and raised her shoulders. She looked directly at the men—one and then the other. "I'm Mrs. Nakahara. What may I do for you?" she asked.

The man removed his hat. "Is Mr. Nakahara at home?" he asked.

"Is there anything I can—"

"My name is Agent Carson. This is Agent Aldo. As I said, we're from the FBI. We need to speak to your husband." Now there was more force in his voice.

Father had appeared by then, behind Mother. He was wearing his work clothes, a bulky wool jacket over overalls. He had taken off his boots, and in his stocking feet, he seemed to shrink before the men.

"Are you Mr. Nakahara?"

Father nodded, or maybe bowed just slightly.

"Do you publish a Japanese-language newspaper?"

He nodded again.

"We understand you keep close ties to people in Japan. Is that right?"

Mother said, "He doesn't speak much English, Mr. Carson. He has relatives in Japan, and he writes letters to them now and then, but his ties are all to this country now. He has lived here for more than thirty years."

"Well, that's what *you* say," Agent Aldo said. "But he's on our list. Tell him we're arresting him."

Yuki's breath stopped.

Father spoke better English than Mother was letting on, and he had surely understood the word "arrest," but he didn't move, didn't show any reaction.

Mother's hands had jumped, as though of their own accord, but then she grasped them together. Yuki saw her blink, knew she was fighting tears, but her voice was strong when she said, "I don't understand. What are the charges against my husband?"

"I told you, he's on a list. Tell him he's got to come with us."

"But you can't arrest him for no reason. He hasn't done anything wrong." She took a step sideways, placing herself in front of her husband.

"If that's the case, he has nothing to worry about,"

Agent Carson said. "But for right now, he has to come with us."

"Where will you take him?"

"I'm sorry, ma'am, it's not our job to explain everything to you. We've been sent to bring him in. I guess you'll hear from others who can tell you the details."

"Must he go with you right now? Can't he—"

"I'm afraid we're going to take him now. We do need to search your house, however. I want you and your son to sit right here in the living room while we put your husband in our car. Then one of us will come back and do the search."

"Search for what?"

"Look, lady," Aldo said, "you don't ask the questions. We do. Sit down, you and your son. Do you have other children?"

"Yes. Two daughters and another son."

"Where are they?"

"Not home from school yet. They come on a bus."

"And what about you?" He looked at Yuki. "Don't you go to school?"

"I get out earlier, so I help my father on the farm. We work hard. We're *Americans*. We—"

"Stop right there. I don't want to hear all that," Aldo said.

Carson put up his hand, as if to say "That's enough" to his partner. "We're going to ask you to go with us now, Mr. Nakahara," he said.

"I must change clothes," Father said.

"No, sir, you don't need to do that. They'll have clothes for you where you're going. Were those your shoes on the porch?"

"Yes."

"Just grab them as we go out. That's all you'll need."

Agent Aldo stepped forward and took hold of Mr. Nakahara's arm. "Come with us now," he said. He pulled on Father's elbow and Father stumbled forward, then caught his balance and looked at Mother. "Where am I going?" he asked in Japanese. Yuki had attended Japanese language school when he was younger. He didn't speak Japanese fluently, but he understood most things his parents said.

Mother didn't answer her husband. She stepped toward Carson. "You can't do this. This is America. You must tell us what he is charged with."

"You speak English very well," Carson said in an almost friendly tone. "How long have you lived in our country?"

"Most of my life. It's my country too."

"You're an enemy alien, ma'am. Not a citizen."

"My children are citizens. How can you take their father from them?"

"We don't get into all that. We just—"

"I learned about American laws in school. You must tell my husband which law he's broken. You cannot take him away without doing that."

"Actually, in time of war, in a war zone, under direction of our government, we can arrest those who may be a danger to others. This area has been designated a war zone by the government, and your husband has been listed as a probable spy. We don't have to tell you all that, but now we have. Please get out of our way and let us do our job." He took hold of Father's other arm, at the elbow, and the two men led him toward the door, Father not resisting.

"You must not do this," Mother was saying, her voice now desperate. She rushed ahead, got between the men and the front door. "My husband is not a danger to anyone. Can't you see that?"

Aldo turned suddenly and stepped close to Mother. "That's enough, lady. Your husband's a sneaky little slant-eyed *Jap*. That's all we need to know." He glared into her eyes, as if to see how she might react, but Mrs. Nakahara's face only hardened. "On Sunday a bunch of sneaky slant-eyed Japs—just like him—bombed our country. His crime is, he's on their side, not ours. And we're not going to let him make contact with his buddies who are waging a war against us. Now, get out of our way or I'll take you in with him." He used his forearm to sweep her aside.

Yuki had watched all this, not knowing what to do or say, but he finally reacted. As the men took Father out the door, he followed, and then he hurried in front of Agent Carson and stood his ground. "Listen, sir, we run a business here. We grow fruits and vegetables and sell them at a stand down on the highway. I think you've gotten the wrong idea about us somehow. Is there someone we could talk to? I think this could all be straightened out in a few minutes. My father has a little newspaper that he sends out to the old-timers from Japan around here, but that's all it is. He doesn't bother anyone at all. He's no troublemaker."

It was Aldo who answered. "Oh, I see. I'm glad you cleared that up for us. But you know what? You're a sneaky little slant-eyed Jap yourself, and I don't trust you any more than your traitor of a dad. Now, shut your mouth and go back in the house."

"But there's no need for this, sir. Isn't there someone I can talk to?"

"Yeah. Talk to Mr. Hirohito, the emperor of Japan. See what he can do for you. Now, get out of my way."

Yuki's anger suddenly fired. "You can't treat us like this!" he yelled into Aldo's face.

Aldo slammed both hands into Yuki's chest, sent him stumbling backward. In his rage, Yuki was about to charge the man, but he heard his father's voice, not loud, but firm. "No!"

Yuki stopped at the command, but mostly because he knew that he was only making things worse.

"*Shikata ga nai,*" Father said.

Yuki hated that idea, "it can't be helped." It was

something his father believed and often said. It was the Japanese way of thinking—the old way. Yuki was too American for such acceptance. And yet, there really was nothing he could do. He stepped aside.

Carson grabbed Father's boots, and the two men pushed past Yuki, then opened the car door and forced Father into the backseat. Aldo stayed outside by the car, apparently to make sure that Father didn't try to make a run for it. Carson returned to the house, and he systematically worked his way through the five rooms while Yuki sat with his mother, his arm around her shoulders. All that strength she had tried to show was gone now and she was weeping, her hands over her face.

"I knew this was coming," Yuki said. "All Father thinks about is Japan. I told him to burn all the Japanese stuff he has around the house, but he wouldn't do it."

"How could he do that?"

"The same way a lot of people have been doing."

Yuki had talked to his friend Shigeo Omura about the things happening in California these last few days, since Japan had bombed Pearl Harbor and war had been declared. At lunch on Tuesday, Shig had whispered to him, "They're rounding up anyone who's considered a community leader. Your dad's known—because of his newspaper. He's got to throw out that Buddhist shrine he keeps in your house. My parents have gotten rid of everything in our house that looks Japanese."

Yuki had told his father what he needed to do, but Father had said nothing, done nothing. It was always his way. A son didn't tell a father what to do.

"My father's not like yours," Yuki had told Shig. But he decided not to explain what he meant by that. Instead, he asked, "How are kids treating you?"

Yuki and Shig had carried their lunches to school in paper bags. When Yuki was younger, his mother had prepared him a Japanese bento box, with rice and fish, but kids had turned up their noses at the smell. In high school, he and Shig had switched to bologna sandwiches and apples, like everyone else. But this week, since the attack on Pearl Harbor, they had sat in a corner of the lunchroom, at the end of a table, away from others.

"They stare at me," Shig said. "No one's ever paid any attention to me before, and they're not saying anything to me now, but all week, I've seen them looking at me—like I'm not the guy I was before."

Yuki nodded. "It's been the same for me," he said. "Some boy I don't even know said I should 'go back to Japan'—like I've ever been there. But he didn't say it to my face. He whispered it behind me in the hallway and then he slipped into the crowd so he didn't have to look me in the eye."

Two girls approached the table with their lunches, but they stopped short and turned away, leaving the table mostly empty in the crowded lunchroom. Yuki thought of welcoming them, but he knew that although it would have been all right the week before, it wasn't now.

"People *like* you, Yuki," Shig said. "You're popular. They'll get over the shock before long, and they'll know you haven't changed. But me, I'm just the little shrimp I've always been. The war only makes things worse."

"Hey, you're the best second baseman this school's ever had. The guys who play with us know that."

"That doesn't matter anymore."

Yuki and Shig had played baseball together for many years. Yuki had always played shortstop and Shig second base, and they had become a great double-play combination. It was true that Shig was really small—only about five feet tall—and he was quiet, so maybe that was why people didn't notice him around the school. The ballplayers had always teased him about having no strike zone and about wearing glasses. But Shig was smart, and when he let loose a little, he was funny. He let Yuki get all the attention and do most of the talking, but when Yuki was struggling, especially with his stern father, Shig would always listen.

What Yuki also knew was that he was going to need Shig more than ever now that the white kids were turning away from them. He had always considered himself friends with people of all races. He had played sports, gone to dances, hung out at soda fountains, and girls had liked to dance with him because he did the jitterbug so well. He had bought himself an old jalopy of a car and had taken girlfriends to the movies, worn the latest styles, been a regular guy. Now—overnight—he was "the enemy."

The lunchroom was full of noise, the same as ever. Maybe a war had started, but kids were talking and laughing the way they always had. But now Yuki could see three Japanese American girls he knew headed for the table where he and Shig were sitting. This was becoming an island for the Japanese students, and yet, that was the last thing any of them wanted.

"Will you stick with me, Yuki?" Shig asked.

Yuki was taking a drink from his Coke bottle. He put it down. "What do you mean, Shig? Of course I'll—"

"It's going to be tougher now. This war might last a long time. If people are going to stare at me all day, every day, I'm going to go crazy. I need someone I can be 'normal' around."

"Hey, I need the same thing. We'll look out for each other."

But now, at home, with the arrest of Yuki's father, things had taken a new turn. It struck Yuki that he was going to have to provide for his family. Maybe he would have to drop out of school. He glanced at his mother, saw how devastated she was. "Don't worry," he told her. "We'll be all right. I'll keep the farm going." But Yuki knew the truth: *Everything* had changed, and nothing was going to be easy.

Agent Carson carried out a lot of stuff: copies of the newspaper Father published, a ceremonial sword that Father had brought with him from Japan, some paper lanterns, a set of binoculars and a flashlight, some letters written in Japanese, and even the Buddha statue from Father's shrine. Then, for some reason, Carson came back and got the tabletop radio that sat on a kitchen shelf. "Why take our radio?" Mother asked, but Carson didn't answer.

"I didn't find any guns. Are there any on your property? Maybe out in that shed?"

"We don't own guns," Mrs. Nakahara said. "We have no need for them."

"I'll just say this: You better not be lying. If you're caught with weapons at any time, your husband won't be the only one locked up." He touched the brim of his hat. "We'll be going now. Be sure to follow the new curfew laws—don't go out after eight o'clock in the evening. I'm sure you'll hear from your husband at some point. Thank you for your cooperation." With the radio under his arm, he walked out to the car.

Yuki got up and watched. He could see his father hunched in the backseat, staring ahead. The agents drove away, the car once again raising a plume of dust. Mother stood up, came to Yuki. He took her in his arms and she sobbed against his shoulder. "There must be someone I can talk to," Yuki said. "We have to get this straightened out."

"No one will listen to us, Yuki. You know that."

But Yuki didn't want to believe it. He was an American, a citizen, and his family was loyal to the United States. They were farmers, churchgoers; they operated a produce business and paid their taxes. Father may have kept his shrine and he may have retained his love for Japan, but he was grateful for all he had been able to achieve here. And Mother was a "church lady," a Methodist, who spoke English more correctly than most, with no Japanese accent at all. What more could people expect of them?

CHAPTER 2

April 1943

Yuki held Keiko's hand as they walked from the dance floor. The dining hall where the teen dances were held on Friday nights was much too warm, and Yuki had been trying out all his jitterbug steps, so sweat was beading up on his forehead and his shirt was sticking to his back. But Keiko looked pleased with herself, and Yuki had the feeling that she was pleased with him, too. She was two years younger than he was, and she had always been "Shig's little sister" to him—but she had grown up a lot in the last year, and recently it had struck him that she was probably the cutest girl in the whole camp.

Yuki spotted Shig standing by the wall. There was a big crowd tonight, and there were plenty of girls to dance with, but so far Shig hadn't asked any of them. That was nothing new. Shig just wasn't confident in his dancing, and especially in his ability to talk with girls. In spite of all the changes in their lives—the roundup of Japanese Americans on the coast, and the transport to this desert camp in Utah—Shig was pretty much the same kid he had always been.

"Hey," Shig said, "you two can *swing* it. I didn't know you had it in you, Keiko."

Keiko smiled, showing her dimples—which Yuki loved to look at. She had an innocent, round face and quick eyes. And her skin, flushed a little now, was delicate, perfect. "I've been practicing with my girlfriends," she said, "but Yuki knows more tricks. Did you see him throw me in the air?" She raised her arms to imitate the way he had lifted her.

"Hey, *everyone* saw him do that," Shig said. "You better be careful, little girl—and keep your dress down."

That obviously embarrassed Keiko. She slapped Shig across his shoulder and walked away.

"Don't give her a hard time," Yuki told Shig.

"I'm not. I was just teasing her. But what's going on with you two? Do you like my little sister?"

"Hey, she's cute as a bug's ear. What's not to like?" The truth was, Yuki liked her a lot more than he wanted to admit. He had flirted with her at lunch one day, and the joking had evolved into a long conversation. Since then, they had talked almost every day. What he had realized was that she was not only cute, but smart, and surprisingly thoughtful about life. A lot of Japanese girls thought they had to be quiet and deferential around men—the way their mothers were—but Keiko wasn't afraid to express her opinions and even disagree with Yuki at times.

"Yuki, she's only sixteen."

"I know. But you know what? When I get back from the war, she's going to be all grown up. And who knows, maybe I'll grow up myself." He put his hands on Shig's shoulders and pretended to be serious. "The way I see it, your family would be *greatly* honored if I married her. By then, I'll be better looking than ever—if that's even possible—and I'll have about fifty medals on my chest."

"Or maybe a bullet hole between your eyes."

"Not me. I'm quick as a jackrabbit. No one's going to shoot me." He made a little sideways jump and ducked his head.

The music had started again—the Mills Brothers singing "Glow Worm." It was just a record in a jukebox, but it was loud in the low-ceilinged building. The dancers were all Japanese American, but the "American" part was the obvious part. Most of the girls were wearing bobby socks and saddle oxfords or penny loafers, and cute cotton print dresses or stylish skirts and blouses. The guys had arrived in sports jackets and ties, but most had set their coats aside by now.

"Come here a second, Yuki," Shig said. He walked to the nearby entrance and stepped out into the night air. It was April, and lately the days had been warm in the high-elevation Utah desert, but nights were still cold. That cool air felt good to Yuki as he stepped outside. "Have you made up your mind for sure?" Shig asked. "Are you really going to enlist?"

"You know I am. And so are you."

"Maybe. I'm still not sure."

"You've got to go with me, Shig. You can't break up the ol' double-play combination."

But Yuki had sounded a little too serious, even to himself. He looked up at the stars in the darkening sky. As much as he tried to hide it, he had a hard time fighting back his fear of leaving his mother, going off to war. Japanese Americans were not being drafted into the military like everyone else, but they were now being recruited, and some were choosing to sign up. For most of the guys in camp, it was not an easy decision.

Yuki and Shig now lived in the Central Utah Relocation Center, known as Topaz. After Yuki's father had been arrested during those final days of 1941, the Nakaharas had received no word from him for quite some time. He finally wrote that he had been hauled off to a prison in Montana. He still hadn't been charged with a crime, but he offered no hope that he would return before the end of the war. From then on, Yuki had felt the full weight of responsibility for his family, of making sure that they at least had food on their table.

Then, in March 1942, Yuki had seen a man pasting a sheet of paper on a telephone pole in downtown Berkeley. He had an idea what the sign might say, but he still felt a stab of pain when he read the words. Executive Order 9066 had been passed by Congress and signed into law by President Roosevelt. All Japanese who lived in the West Coast states—whether citizens or not—were required to register with the government. What followed in April was worse. With only a few days' warning, more than 110,000 AJA—Americans of Japanese ancestry—were commanded to assemble at various sites for "relocation." The order stated that they should bring only what they could carry, which meant one or two suitcases and the clothes they were wearing.

Mother, and especially Yuki's sisters, May and Kay, had been devastated. His brother, Mick, had been silent but clearly resentful. Lots of rumors were going around by then, but no one knew where this relocation would take them. All Yuki knew was that he had to hold things together, act confident whether he was or not, and offer his family what consolation he could think of.

The Nakaharas' farm was only leased, since *Issei*—first-generation Japanese immigrants—were not allowed to own land. Still, the tractor, truck, and equipment couldn't just sit on a farm that the family would no longer occupy. Everything had to be sold immediately. Father had left a little money in a bank, but Japanese accounts had been frozen by the government and Mother couldn't access any of her own money. Yuki was baffled that such a thing could happen in the "land of the free."

The morning after seeing the posted order, Yuki had picked up the *Oakland Tribune* and read the headline JAPS GIVEN EVACUATION ORDERS HERE. The term "Jap" was not new, but it had always been considered disrespectful. Now it was being printed in the newspapers.

Throughout the spring, Yuki had tried to manage the farm and still go to school every day. His mother wouldn't hear of him dropping out. He had to be the one to accept forty dollars for a tractor that was worth three hundred, and courteously thank the man who had started out by offering thirty. A lot of their other things—furniture, kitchen items, books—had to be stacked in a barn loft, and there was no telling what would happen to any of it. Mrs. Nakahara was furious, but she told her children as they prepared to leave their house, "Dress in your Sunday clothes, and hold your heads up. The government is shaming itself, but we never will."

Yuki lived with a barely controlled anger, but he kept thinking ahead. When the war was over, he had to be ready to make a life for himself and for his family. It was obvious to him that he had to avoid all appearance of being anything but a loyal American.

At first, Yuki's family, along with Shig's, had been housed in stinking, fly-infested horse stables at the

Tanforan Racetrack in San Bruno, south of San Francisco. Then, after a few months of that humiliation, they had been transported by train to Utah, where barracks covered only in tar paper had been quickly thrown together. Each barracks was divided into six small rooms. The Nakaharas had to squeeze into primitive quarters, twelve feet wide and twenty feet long, with no partitions. Most mortifying were the public toilets. In each was a long board with holes cut in it, and no dividers in between. Yuki's sisters would sometimes wait most of the day to find a moment when they could sneak into the women's side alone.

The desert of central Utah was fiercely hot in the summer, and then the "internees"—just a nice word for "prisoners," as far as Yuki was concerned—survived suffocating dust storms in the fall. The constant wind blew right through the loosely constructed walls and floors. Winter on the high plateau was brutal, with no insulation in the walls and only a small coal stove for heat—and coal in short supply. Yuki and his family tried to make the best of their situation by building furniture from boxes and waste lumber and by planting a garden in the alkaline soil, but nothing felt normal. Most everyone housed in the camp had lived all their lives in the lush San Francisco Bay area. Now they were stuck in this remote place, on ugly, arid land. The nearest town, Delta, was fifteen miles away, and around the camp was nothing but sagebrush and greasewood. To Yuki, it looked like a broad stretch of nothingness.

Schools had been established in the camp by fall, and now, in the spring of 1943, Yuki was about to complete his senior year of high school. Teachers had been recruited from the area, and a few had been excellent, but others had hardly known their subjects. What discouraged Yuki most, however, was knowing that going on to college would have little or no value, since most AJA would not be able to get jobs in the careers they chose. Who was going to hire a Japanese teacher or engineer?

And yet, in spite of all that, the young men were now being recruited to enlist as soldiers—to fight for America. During the winter, Yuki and Shig had both turned eighteen, so they knew they would have to make a choice. For many of the men in the camp, the idea of defending the same country that had taken away their freedom was unthinkable. *Nisei*—second-generation Japanese Americans—supposedly possessed full citizenship, but they found themselves surrounded by tall barbed-wire fences and guard towers. Everyone in camp knew the story of the older man who had wandered out toward the fence one day and been shot and killed by a guard. The guard claimed that the man had been trying to crawl under the fence—but the bullet had struck him in the chest. He had obviously been standing up, facing the guard. And the question was, where could he have gone anyway? Out into the desert? Government spokesmen liked to say that the AJA were being kept in camps for their own safety, but if that were the case, the people asked, why were the machine guns in the guard towers pointed inward, not outward?

Standing outside now, Yuki lowered his gaze from the stars to the distant mountains—just a hint of a purple silhouette against an almost dark sky. Lately he had felt as though he were hanging over a cliff, his fingerhold slipping away. "Shig, we have to join up," he said. "It's the only way we'll ever be respected in this country."

"I'm not sure it will make any difference."

"You've listened to too many of those 'no, no' guys. But look what's happened to them."

Earlier in the year, a controversy had broken out at Topaz and the other camps. The War Relocation Authority had made an attempt to discover how many of the interned people were willing to proclaim their loyalty to America. Imprisoning people based only on their race was not easy to justify, and government officials were looking for a way to release some of the internees and avoid the expense of housing and feeding them. The questionnaire, however, asked two questions that bothered many AJA. Question 27 asked those of draft age whether they would be willing to serve in the military, and question 28 asked whether they were willing to swear allegiance to the United States and forswear allegiance to Japan. Yuki was shocked when he read the second question. He was an American citizen. Why should he have to swear off allegiance to a foreign country? All the same, he wrote "yes" to both questions, knowing that a "no" would give the wrong impression.

As it turned out, those who had written "no" to the two questions were labeled "disloyals" and transferred to a camp in the California desert where they would be carefully watched and segregated from "loyals." This way of handling things had created bitterness even in those who had answered "yes" or who had left the questions blank, and Yuki knew that Shig had struggled when one of their good friends—who certainly was no danger to anyone—had been hauled away.

"I know how you feel about Kenji," Yuki continued. "I feel the same way. But—"

"It's not just that. And I'm not a chicken. But I'm not sure I want to die for people who hate my guts."

"We won't die. We'll come home war heroes, and those same people will be thanking us."

"I doubt that. You know what people called us when we worked in the beet fields."

Yuki and Shig and a lot of others had been allowed to go off camp to help harvest sugar beets—and they had worked hard. But several times, people had driven past the farm and yelled, "Filthy Japs!" And when Yuki and Shig had tried to go to a movie, the manager—a pudgy young guy who looked about the right age to be serving in the army himself—had stood at the door and said, "We don't allow Japs in here, so move on."

Yuki had laughed and said, "Listen, friend, we're from California. We're Americans, just like you. I'm a Methodist, for crying out loud. A Boy Scout."

The young fellow had looked surprised for a moment, as though he hadn't expected Yuki to sound like other teenagers. "Well, people still don't want to sit next to you in a dark theater," he said, but he sounded less adamant than he had at first.

"What do they think? That we're going to sneak up and cut their throats?" Yuki bent over and pretended to draw a knife across someone's neck. "Hey, we're out there digging sugar beets—for the war effort—and we love America, the same as you. I'm going to join the army as soon as they'll let me."

The guy seemed disarmed by that. He stared at Yuki for a time, and then he merely said, "Well, anyway, I can't let you in. That's what the owner told me."

"That's all right. We understand. We're not trouble-makers."

The man had nodded, actually seemed halfway friendly, and Yuki had felt good about the conversation. It was what he had been doing for years. When he had worked at his father's produce stand, he had always been able to tell when shoppers were hesitant to deal with a Japanese clerk, so Yuki had learned to go out of his way to be helpful, to chat with people about the weather, or about sports—which he knew as well as anyone—and he almost always felt that he broke through with people. Some became steady customers and would laugh and talk with him whenever they came in.

But Shig had never possessed Yuki's ease with people. When he had played baseball, the chatter started when he came to bat. Players on opposing teams called him "shrimp," and "four eyes," and sometimes, behind his back, "that little Jap." Yuki had always taken any abuse or teasing he had faced and had been able to toss it back at the white guys, but Shig had never been able to do that.

"I'll tell you what else makes me mad," Shig continued. "They're making up a whole regiment of *Nisei* soldiers. White guys refuse to fight alongside us."

"I know. But it's not so strange if guys like to be around their own people. I hate this camp, but it's kind of nice to be on our own, where we all understand each other. The trouble is, sooner or later we have to get past all that stuff—and just not think about what race we are. For now, though, the way I look at it, if we're the best regiment in the whole army, we'll *demand* respect—and we'll get it."

"And what makes you so sure we're going to be that good?"

Yuki had to think about that. He tucked his hands in his pockets. He didn't like the desert, but he did love the amazing smear of stars across the night sky, and that's what he looked at now.

"Shig," he said, after a time, "I'll tell you how I feel about giving my all to this war." But he hesitated, still a little unsure he could say the words. "I keep saying that the government had no right to put my father in prison. And that's true. He's not a spy, and he's not a traitor. But there's something I've always known about him. He's not an American the way my mother is, and he never will be. His heart has always stayed with Japan. I don't want to be like that. If I want to be respected, I have to give over my loyalty to *this* country, entirely. The white guys are signing up and going out to risk their lives to protect America. If I don't enlist, I'm the same as my father—Japanese at heart."

Shig didn't speak for a while. Yuki knew that Shig's father was much more American in his thinking. He was a farmer, but he raised flowers and marketed them as a wholesaler. He dealt with businesses all through the West. He had no thoughts of returning to Japan. Shig didn't have to feel ashamed of him.

Finally Shig said, "I know what you're saying. I'm an American and I want to do my part. But would we be 'protecting' America? The Japanese navy is already retreating. They'll never drop bombs on the mainland, and how's Hitler supposed to attack us over here?"

"Shig, the Nazis could still take over all of Europe, and

then what happens to our world? Hitler is rounding up Jews and—"

"And putting them in camps. How's that worse than what our country is doing to us?"

It was the question a lot of young Japanese American men were asking.

"I just like to believe that Americans will think this all over sooner or later, and finally get it right. But that will never happen under a dictator like Hitler. He'll never stop until someone stops him, and he thinks that anyone who isn't blond and blue-eyed is worthless. If Germany controls the world, what kind of world will it be?"

Shig nodded but didn't say anything.

"Am I right?"

"Yeah. I think so. But I still have to make up my own mind."

Yuki had been too serious for too long. He didn't want to argue with Shig. "I'll tell you why *I* am going to be a great soldier," he said. "I'll fight the way I dance—smooth but *snappy*." Yuki grinned and gave Shig a little punch in the shoulder, and then he began his jitterbug steps, even pretended to swing a girl under his arm. "You're sure going to be embarrassed if I'm your brother-in-law and a big-shot war hero and you have to admit that you spent the war sitting here in this dumpy camp."

"Hey, stay away from Keiko. I don't want to be related to you." But Shig was finally laughing.

"You have to enlist, Shig. We're a team. Quit thinking so much. Let's go see what the world looks like—and shoot a few Nazis while we're at it."

"Papa says I need to graduate from high school first."

"Don't worry about that. I talked to the camp director. He said we're close enough. He'll let us have our diplomas right now. So what other excuses do you have?"

Shig hesitated, and then he said, "I want to go, Yuki. But I do need to talk to my parents one more time."

"Okay. But you're eighteen. You don't need their permission."

"I know. But I want it."

Yuki nodded. That was something he did understand. But he was enlisting—in spite of what his mother had been telling him.

Yuki pointed to the door. "For now, let's give some girls the chance to dance with us. It's what they're dreaming about in there, and we can't let them down."

Yuki was still laughing when he reached for the door handle, but then he stopped. He joked too much sometimes and he knew it. There was something Shig needed to know. He turned back and said, "I need you, buddy. We promised to stick together forever. I feel like I've got to enlist, but I just can't do it without you."

Shig nodded. "I know," he said. "I feel the same way."

CHAPTER 3

Yuki needed to talk to his mother. Still, it took him another couple of days to build up his courage and to find a few minutes with her alone. He and his mother and siblings all slept in the same room on army cots. At night, Mother would hang blankets on ropes strung across the room to separate the boys from herself and her daughters, and then, after everyone made their way back from the bathhouse in the morning and got dressed, the blankets came down, just so the room would seem more open. But that left few opportunities for Yuki to be alone with his mother. What was worse, with the walls between rooms not rising all the way to the ceiling, anything said could be heard at least in the next room, and loud talk—angry talk—would fill the entire barracks.

On Sunday morning, Yuki and his family wore their best clothes and walked to the building where the

Protestant church services were held—just another tar paper structure, like all the barracks. Yuki had never been terribly enthusiastic about sermons, and this was a day when he paid little attention to the minister. His mind was on the things he would have to tell Mother and what she was likely to say in response.

Yuki never knew whether he was religious or not. Sometimes his mother asked him to pray for the family, and he used the same Christian words he had heard her use, but he never prayed on his own, and he wasn't sure he knew what he expected from prayer. He didn't know much about Buddhism, and his father's willingness to accept his fate so easily bothered Yuki at times, but Father never asked much for himself and made the most of his situation in life. That was something Yuki admired.

After church, the Nakaharas walked back to their barracks. They stayed on the gravel path to keep out of the alkaline dust, which floated up with every step and then settled on pant legs and skirts. Yuki's brother, Mick—whose actual name was Mikeo—was sixteen now, and he was even less tolerant of sermons than Yuki was. He had walked quickly ahead, probably to get his necktie off as soon as possible. Yuki's sisters, May and Kay, who were fourteen and twelve, walked ahead too. Yuki's father had wanted Japanese names for his children, and Mother had agreed to name their daughters

Amaya and Kayo, but Father was the only one who called them that.

Now seemed the time, walking alone with Mother, for Yuki to tell her that he had made his decision. "I know this will not be a surprise to you," he started. "We've talked about this before. But I need to tell you, tomorrow morning I'm going to enlist in the army. I don't know how soon I'll be leaving, but it won't be long."

Mrs. Nakahara stopped. Yuki took one more step and then stopped too, and he looked back. They were standing in the gravel path between a row of barracks, and his mother's face looked as stark as the colorless ground around them. She had strong emotions, and she could be intense at times, but more commonly, she was formal and correct. Yuki always believed that he must be respectful, even careful, in the way he spoke to her.

"You must receive your father's permission first," Mother said.

"I've written twice now and told him what I want to do. He only writes back to *you* and tells you that I shouldn't do it."

"And you will defy him?"

"Mother, I don't need his signature. I'm eighteen. I can enlist on my own."

She stared into his eyes. She was wearing her purple dress, her pretty church dress, and a little black pillbox hat. Her white-gloved hands moved to her hips now, and she stood before him, firm. "You have not been raised to say such things, Yukus. You know better. Your father may be away, but he is still your father."

"This is something I *must* do, Mother, not just something I want to do. Father will be called a criminal all his life if I don't change people's minds about us. I can bring back honor to our family."

"You think I'm not so Japanese as your father, Yukus, and it's true, I'm not. But a child should honor his father. That is Japanese, but it's Christian, too."

Mother began to walk again, and Yuki walked alongside her, their shoes crunching in the gravel. He wasn't sure what he could say next, but he knew how his mother thought. She was eleven years younger than her husband. She had married him when she was nineteen. He had come to America earlier to earn enough money to return to Japan and buy land there. Mother's parents had considered Father a good prospect, a farmer who was well established. Like so many of the *Issei*, Mother's parents had thought of returning to Japan themselves. But Mother had been only four when she came to America, and she remembered nothing about Japan. All the same, as she had admitted to Yuki, she never felt fully accepted by people in California. Maybe it was that isolation, Yuki thought, that had caused her to keep to the ways of her family. She had complied with her parents' wishes and agreed to marry Hasakao Nakahara.

Mother had told Yuki that as a little girl she hadn't known she was different. The white children had been kind to her for the most part, and some of the little boys had thought she was pretty. But when she reached her teen years, she realized that she was always kept at a distance. It seemed to Yuki that she held back her own instincts—her American way of thinking—when it came to dealing with Father. He treated her like a daughter in many ways. He probably let her have her freedom in the home more than his own father would have done, but when it came to decisions about the children, about most anything significant, he spoke with authority and expected his wife to obey. And he expected the same of his children.

When Yuki and his mother arrived at the barracks, Mother asked Yuki to put up a blanket and then she slipped behind it to change her clothes. Yuki took his suit off and hung it up. There was no closet, only pegs to hang things on. Still, he was careful to hang the trousers correctly, as he had been taught, so as not to ruin the crease Mother had ironed into them.

The other children had dressed in their play clothes already and run off to dinner. The dining hall setting had made it possible for young people to eat with friends, and that's what they chose to do. A family dinner simply didn't happen now. There was always a long line on Sundays, and Mick and the girls liked to get there as early as possible. Much of the food served at the dining hall was detestable to Japanese tastes, but the cooks had to do with what they had, so all too often they served liver or tripe, and more often than not, they served mashed potatoes. Yuki and his family much preferred rice and fresh vegetables, but neither was available most of the time. Lately, however, and especially on Sundays, the cooks sometimes served fried chicken, and most of the people in camp liked that.

"Mother, listen, I want you to know—"

"Don't say it. If you plan to defy me and your father, simply do it. But don't make me listen to any more of your noble talk about serving your country."

"How can you say that, Mom? I—"

"Don't call me 'Mom.' Your father hates that."

"The last I checked, he's not around to hear what I say."

"And that is the point, isn't it?" Mother was standing with her head high. Yuki admired that, and he loved his mother more than anyone in the world. He didn't want to hurt her, or defy her, but he doubted, really, that she felt the same as Father did. She was taking his side because she felt she had to. Surely she already knew what Yuki was going to do.

"I have to do this, Mother."

"And what am I to do?"

Her voice had risen, and Yuki knew what she feared:

that others in the building would hear the two of them arguing. She motioned for Yuki to move outside, and then she stepped ahead of him out the door. She walked well away from the building, out into the alkaline dust, and then she turned and looked at him. "I don't know what to do about May. She eats with children her own age in the dining room, stays away from me most of the time, and spends her days with those same children—boys and girls together."

"They're not children, Mother. They're growing up."

"They *are* children. And they have taught her to talk back to me. When I ask her where she's been and what she's been doing, she won't answer. She told me last week that she didn't have to report everything she does to me. What would your father say to that?"

"You know what he would say. But from what I know, she isn't doing anything bad."

"Is she kissing those boys? Are they touching her? How do I know? It may be worse than that. I think you know what's happened to the Fuji girl. Her mother's heart is broken."

"May isn't like that. She—"

"I don't know what she is, and now you want to leave me and let me figure out everything for myself. We won't have your money, Yukus. You've gone out and worked, and that bought clothes for your brother and sisters and helped us get a little furniture. What now?"

"Mick can work. He should have been working all along."

Mother looked back toward the barracks as a family walked out. She bowed her head and greeted them, wished them a pleasant Sunday. Yuki knew she was afraid of their noticing that the two were arguing, but Yuki didn't care nearly so much about that. "Mom, I know this is hard. I'm not saying that it won't be. But you told those FBI agents back in California that they shouldn't arrest Father because we're Americans. Do you remember that? How can you expect me to stay out of the war? We can't have it both ways. I'm an American, and I'm going to prove it. White families are saying good-bye to their sons, and they don't have a choice."

"And what did those agents say about us? We're 'slant-eyed little Japs.' How can we be Americans when people think of us that way?"

"There's a better question than that, Mother. What will make them change their minds? That's what I intend to do, starting tomorrow morning." Mother looked doubtful, but she didn't respond. "Think about this," Yuki said. "All my life, Father has taught me never to shame my family, to be a man of honor. He doesn't want me to leave you now, but what would he have done if the emperor had called him as a young man to fight for Japan?"

"You know what he would have done. He would have

served. But everything is different here. No one called him names in Japan, and no one put him in prison."

"That's why some things have to change. But I still have to serve my country. It's a matter of honor. Father ought to understand that better than anyone."

Mother was finally looking down, no longer taking him on with her eyes. "I understand, Yukus. You must follow your own sense of duty. But must it be now? We have no idea whether your father will ever be released. We have no farm to go back to. What will I do if I don't have your help when we finally get out of this place?"

"Mick has to grow up. That's all. When the war is over, I'll come back to you and we'll go back to California."

"Yes. And what if you don't come back? How will I . . ."

She broke down. Yuki had seen her weep before, but never in a place like this, out where people might walk by. Sobs were breaking from deep inside her.

"Mother, I won't take chances. I promise you that."

"You can't promise any such thing. War *is* chance. And all you talk about is coming home a hero, showing how brave you are. You'll be killed, Yukus, and you are my firstborn son."

She was still sobbing, and Yuki took her into his arms. "It's a war we have to win, Mother. And I have to help fight it. Can't you be proud of me for that?"

"Pride is a bad thing, Yukus. It's an American idea that it's good."

"I still think you're proud of me."

Mother looked into his eyes, the tears streaming down her face. "Yes," she finally said. "I am an American. And I am proud of you. I'm just very, very frightened."

"I know. I am too. But we'll be okay. I'm sure of it."

CHAPTER 4

Yuki met with the recruiter the next morning—he and Shig—and they signed their enlistment papers. Shig had also had a long talk with his mother and father, and they had approved his decision. Shig didn't tell Yuki exactly what he had said, but Yuki assumed he had told them the same kinds of things that Yuki had told his mother.

A week later, Yuki and Shig, along with a couple dozen other *Nisei*, readied themselves to board a bus and travel to Salt Lake City to undergo physical examinations. If they passed, they would be inducted into the United States Army. Shig had admitted to Yuki that he was nervous about that, since he knew he might be rejected for being too short.

Yuki had only laughed. "Don't worry, I'll stretch you before we go in," Yuki told him. "And you can comb your hair up high."

Shig grinned. "I wrote five foot two on the papers we filled out. Maybe they'll just take my word for it."

"And what color did you say your eyes were? Blue?"

"Yeah. And my name's O'Moora. I'm Irish. Didn't you know that?"

"Don't worry about any of that stuff. You're getting in. If they try to turn you down, I'll beat up on somebody."

"Yeah, that'll work."

But now, as the recruits prepared to board the bus and all the families gathered around their sons, there was not much laughter—just lots of quiet talk and some tears. Yuki had spent time with Mick the night before, told him that he had to take on more responsibility, protect his sisters, support his mother. Mick had solemnly promised that he would do his best. He had always held his emotions inside, and he didn't have much to say as the bus started its engine—but when Yuki said "I guess it's time to go," Mick grabbed his big brother, embraced him, and cried. Yuki had always wondered whether Mick even liked him, but he understood what the boy was thinking now. The moment felt like an ending. Yuki had assured his family over and over that he would come back, but it wasn't something he could actually promise. The same thought was surely in everyone's mind: This might be the last time we'll see each other.

Yuki clung to Mick, told him that everything would be all right, but tears were running down his cheeks as he said the words, and he knew that even if he did come home, nothing would ever be the same.

May was more like Mother than she would ever admit. She didn't like to cry in front of people, and even though she usually talked incessantly, she didn't know what to say now. "Where do you think they will send you, Yuki?" she asked, as though she didn't want to say anything that would make her cry.

"I don't know," Yuki said. He took hold of both her shoulders and looked into her face. "I'll be in training for quite a while, and then, who knows? Most people think we'll go to Europe, so we don't have to fight the Japanese."

She nodded. "Be careful, okay?"

"Sure. Don't worry."

"But I do worry," she said, and then all her emotions came pouring out. She wrapped her arms around Yuki and cried hard.

Kay joined the two of them. Her head only came up to May's shoulder, but she wrapped her arms around both Yuki and May as far as she could reach. "Please don't go," she kept saying, over and over.

There was nothing Yuki could tell her, and he could no longer speak anyway. He finally stepped away from May's arms and bent and hugged Kay. He managed to say "I'm sorry," although he hardly knew what he meant.

Mother had done her crying, and she was in a public place now. The bus engine was grumbling and diesel exhaust was in the air. "Go ahead, Yukus. They're calling for you," she said.

"Tell Father good-bye for me. Tell him what I told you. About honor."

She nodded.

Yuki took her in his arms, and he held her for a time. He felt as though he would simply disappear when he got on that bus, never be his mother's boy again.

An army sergeant was calling out, "Come on, boys. We gotta get goin'."

Yuki stepped to the door of the bus, but he looked back one last time. Standing well back, away from the crowd, was Keiko. She was too dressed up for a weekday, in a pretty red dress. When she saw him look toward her, she gave him a brief wave. He wanted to go to her, maybe kiss her good-bye. But he had never kissed her, and at lunch the day before, he had said only that he hoped he would see her again and he hoped she would write to him. He had wanted to say that he was in love with her, and would miss her—wanted even to propose a future together—but that would have been too much, too early in her life, and he hadn't wanted to saddle her with so many expectations. Still, he saw her reach her fingers to her face, whisk away tears from each eye, and his breath stopped. But he still didn't go to her. He waved again, as did she, and then he walked up the steps into the bus.

Yuki found Shig halfway down the aisle, hidden away next to the window, sunk down in his seat. He looked like a little boy, his glasses off, tears on his face. Yuki sat down next to him. "You've got to help me through this," Shig finally managed to say to Yuki.

"We'll help each other. That's the deal."

Then Yuki glanced up to see that his family was still standing by the bus. They all waved when they saw him look at them. And in the distance, Keiko waved again. What he wanted to do, more than anything, was grab Shig and rush for the door. He had been telling himself all this last year that he was a grown-up, that he was ready to go prove himself, but he felt none of that now.

CHAPTER 5

Yuki and Shig, dressed in Class A uniforms, sat up in a train car for two days and two nights on their way to Camp Shelby, near the town of Hattiesburg, Mississippi. They were about to start their basic training. The new army recruits coming in from Salt Lake City had been told to keep their blinds down, so they didn't see much of the nation, except in little peeks. But at the train station in Hattiesburg, Yuki could see why the *Nisei* recruits had been told not to raise the blinds. People stared at them, muttered to each other, and one man actually walked behind Yuki and said what others must have been thinking: "We don't need no Japs to fight our wars for us."

"That feller needs to work on his grammar," Yuki told Shig, and they laughed. But Shig looked tired. He had admitted how homesick he was, and Yuki was feeling the same thing. They were out of their element—breathing water, it seemed—surrounded by a whole world of the unfamiliar. Part of that may have been because the air itself was full of water, steaming over Shig's eyeglasses and causing Yuki to sweat from the slightest effort. And there were new sounds, as though insects had invaded all the trees and were screeching in unison. But mostly it was the grim looks, the accusing eyes. Yuki wanted to yell at people, "Hey, I'm on your side!" but instead he smiled at everyone he passed, wished them a good day. And his friendliness did seem to defuse some of the antagonism. Some nodded back, even smiled a little.

When Yuki and Shig arrived at the military base, they saw lots of soldiers with Asian facial traits and oversized uniforms like their own. The trouble was, the army hadn't figured out how to dress a whole regiment of men—over three thousand soldiers—who were all close to the minimum size requirement. Back in Salt Lake City, Shig had cheated upward, standing almost on his toes, and in truth, Yuki thought the guy measuring him had let him get away with it—probably out of lack of interest more than anything.

The army had decided that white soldiers wouldn't be willing to fight alongside Japanese, so the military high command had segregated the *Nisei* into a separate regiment and quickly tried to spruce up a broken-down military camp for their training. The officers and drill sergeants who processed the new recruits were all white, and they looked like linebackers stolen from football teams—most of them big, all of them loud. They barked and demanded and belittled. Maybe it was what they always did, but Yuki thought they seemed especially disdainful of men who averaged five foot four.

As soon as the recruits walked onto the base, they were commanded to line up and receive their uniforms and equipment. A supply sergeant took one look at Shig and said, "What are you doing here? Come back when you grow up."

Shig was standing in front of a counter, and Yuki had to admit, he did look like a boy in the men's clothing department. His head dropped, which only made him look smaller, but Yuki stepped up next to him. He laughed and put his arm around Shig's shoulders. "I'll tell you what, Sergeant. He's quick as a cat. Don't ever try to slap a ground ball past him, because he'll throw you out at first every time. He's going to be a great soldier."

"Step back right now," the sergeant told Yuki. "You mouth off to me again and you'll be peeling potatoes the rest of the day." Then he looked at Shig. "Now, what girls' size can I get for you?"

Yuki and Shig had only the uniforms they had been provided in Utah. The sergeant now issued them helmets, fatigues, underwear, socks, jackets, combat boots, and various equipment. It was not hard to see that most of it wouldn't fit. The boots Shig received must have been size

6 or 7, and at home he had still worn boys' sizes. "You can stuff something in the toes," Yuki whispered to Shig, but all of this was clearly humiliating to him.

Yuki was certainly no big guy, but at five foot six, he felt pretty good about himself. Even so, the sleeves of the shirt he was given were obviously going to hang over his hands. A lot of recruits had arrived ahead of the Salt Lake men, and the smallest sizes were already gone.

Yuki and Shig purposely stayed together through all of the processing, and that way the two ended up assigned to the same platoon: Second Platoon of Company F of Second Battalion of the 442nd Regimental Combat Team. Almost four thousand men were being trained for the combat team, so they considered themselves lucky to be in the same platoon of about thirty soldiers. They were also assigned to the same hutment, so they grabbed their duffel bags, which now weighed almost as much as they did, and trudged through rows of ugly, boxlike buildings. "Hey, this place reminds me of beautiful Topaz," Yuki told Shig.

"Worse. These buildings are falling apart." The barracks did seem to sag, and a new coat of white paint hadn't covered up their poor condition.

On the shady side of one of the buildings, two soldiers who looked like AJA were sitting on the steps. One of them, a meaty guy, had no shirt on, and neither one was wearing boots. The bigger man was strumming a little stringed instrument and both were singing in some language that sounded half English and half something else.

One of the men—the one without a shirt—called out, "'Ey, you boys katonks?"

Yuki was only too happy to stop and put down his duffel. "Excuse me?" he said.

"Yeh. You katonks, awright. You talk like 'em."

"I'm sorry," Yuki said. "I didn't quite catch what you're—"

"Why you talk like dat?"

"I don't know. It's just the way I—"

"You babooz, dass what. I blow yo head. You wan dat?"

Yuki had no idea what was going on. He glanced at Shig and saw that he was just as perplexed. So Yuki merely said, "Listen, we have to get to our quarters. We'll talk to you again sometime."

But the man put down his instrument and walked straight to Yuki. "We no like katonks," he said. "You t'ink you betta'n us."

The man was bigger than Yuki, much heavier, and he kept coming until he was almost on top of him. Yuki said, as calmly as he could, "My name's Yukus Nakahara. People call me Yuki. This is my friend Shig Omura. We're actually from California, but we spent the last year in Utah. We just arrived here a couple of hours—"

"Don talk like dat. I blow yo head. I min it."

"Listen, we're all in the same army. We might as well—"

The man grabbed Yuki's lapel and pulled him against his bare chest. But just then someone called out, "Shimuzu, let go of that man."

The big fellow did let go. He looked past Yuki toward a soldier—a buck sergeant—walking toward them. But the sergeant was smiling, as though he saw something funny that Yuki didn't see at all. "Don blow no heads, Muki. Dey talk like dat, but dey okay."

"Dey t'ink dey betta'n us."

"No. Dey on'y lolo. Wat can do?"

Muki laughed. "Okay. But tell 'em, stay way." He turned and walked back to his spot in the shade.

"Come on, soldiers," the sergeant said to Yuki and Shig. "I'll help you find your quarters. What unit are you assigned to?"

"F Company, Second Platoon."

"That's what I figured. I heard we were getting new men today. I'm in the same platoon." Then he laughed. "You'll be happy to know, Muki Shimuzu is also in our company. He'll be your 'brudda' before long." He picked up both duffels without any great effort. "You're right down here." As they walked along the road, he said, "I'm Sergeant Matsumoto."

The name was certainly Japanese, but he looked almost Caucasian. He was quite tall, for one thing. His skin was a lighter tone than Yuki's or Shig's, and his eyes looked like a white guy's.

"You didn't know you were katonks, did you?"

"I don't get all this," Shig said. "What was that guy talking about?"

"He's from Hawaii," Sergeant Matsumoto said. "He's a good guy, but he doesn't like mainlanders. Hawaiians say that when they knock down a mainlander, his head makes the sound 'katonk'—like an empty coconut. That's what he was calling you. But the mainlanders call the Hawaiians 'buddhaheads.' It's not really about Buddhism. 'Buta' means 'pig' in Hawaiian. It's like calling a guy 'pigheaded.'"

"But isn't that Muki guy Japanese?"

"Sure. But he grew up in Hawaii. There are close to three thousand AJA from Hawaii on base already, and mainlanders have been coming in these last couple of weeks. It's a clash of cultures like you can't believe."

"Where did you learn to speak like them?" Yuki asked.

"I'm from Hawaii, but I've been living in Wisconsin for a few years. I graduated from college up there. As you can probably guess, my mom is white, so I grew up hearing both dialects. I've always been able to speak like you lolo katonks."

The sergeant stopped outside one of the dilapidated hutments.

"What's 'lolo'?" Yuki asked.

Matsumoto laughed. "It means 'crazy.' And I heard him call you 'babooz.' That means 'stupid.' Just don't take that stuff too seriously."

"But that guy was mad. He wanted to blow my head off."

"'Blow' just means 'punch,' but yeah, he was sort of mad. That's what's going on all over the camp. Fights break out pretty much every day—the buddhaheads and katonks going after each other."

The sergeant sounded smart, and he looked sharp—his uniform neatly pressed and his hair cut short. At the same time, he wasn't like the officers and sergeants who had processed Yuki and Shig at the headquarters building. He didn't seem to care about establishing his authority over them.

"So are all the *Nisei* in camp in the same regiment?"

"That's what they tell us. We'll have to see whether we can ever fight anyone besides each other." But he was smiling, and he didn't seem all that worried. "The Hawaiians don't like me much either. I was already in the army when the war broke out and the army didn't know what to do with guys like me. When they formed the "Four-Four-Two"—that's what the buddhaheads call the 442nd—a lot of us *Nisei* soldiers got assigned here to form the leadership cadre. We're the noncommissioned officers. We'll be the platoon sergeants and squad leaders. To the Hawaiians, the officers are too much like the white men who own the pineapple plantations where a lot of them worked at home. And they certainly don't like having katonks for their sergeants."

"How's all that going to work out when we go into battle?"

"We'll be fine. I'll tell you something. Muki Shimuzu— all the Hawaiians—are good guys. Don't pay too much attention to the pidgin English they speak; a lot of them are well educated. And they're bighearted people. They look after each other, and once a buddhahead is your brudda, he'll do anything for you."

"If he doesn't blow my head first."

Sergeant Matsumoto stepped to the door of the hutment and set down the duffel bags. "I won't see you much during your basic training, but we *will* be brothers when we go to war. For now, though, you're recruits. Don't expect the next sergeant you meet to treat you like human beings."

Yuki didn't like the sound of that. But he was glad he and Shig had met someone who had been around for a while and knew what was going on—and had come along just when they needed him.

As it turned out, the buddhaheads were the least of Yuki's worries. Sergeant Dexter, the drill sergeant for Yuki and Shig's unit, stood before their platoon on the first morning of training. With his chest thrown out, he bellowed: "A lot of people don't believe that you men can be soldiers. Some say that the government just stuck you in the army so the big shots can say they've got nothing against you.

But I'll tell you what. If you *can* be soldiers—which I seriously doubt from the looks of you—you *will* be soldiers." He cursed and spat on the ground. He was not a big man, but he had shoulders like a weightlifter's, and steady blue eyes that didn't blink.

"The next eight weeks will be the worst of your lives. I expect most of you to break down and cry like little boys before I'm finished with you. I'll make you or I'll break you. And I'll tell you why. If you want to get to the battlefront, and want to show you're actually men, you cannot be 'as good' as the white troops. You've got to be a whole lot better."

The tough talk was something right out of movies, and it was all Yuki could do not to smile. Sergeant Dexter seemed to notice this. He walked straight to Yuki, pointed a finger in his face, and shouted, "Don't look so pleased with yourself, little man. I'll break you first."

And then he set out to do it.

He worked the men brutally hard, and he zeroed in on Yuki every chance he got. He called him names, cursed him, told him how worthless he was. Along with all the weapons training and physical workouts, the recruits had to make long, hard marches in the humid heat, not only with heavy packs but with rifles slung over their shoulders. Like Shig, most of the recruits had been issued boots that were too big for them. Everyone had blisters by the end of the first march. All the while, they had to listen to

Sergeant Dexter telling them they weren't men enough to be soldiers. He never called them "Japs," but all the talk about their size amounted to the same thing.

Yuki had never gone through anything so difficult. He came back each day sapped and weary. He would shower and dry off but feel wet again immediately. The hutment never cooled at night; Yuki only slept because he was exhausted. And then Dexter would crash through the door shouting and blowing his whistle, and everything would start again.

Yuki had heard how tough basic training was, but he had told himself he could handle anything. He considered himself in good physical shape, and he wasn't one to let any sort of harassment get the better of him. But this treatment was beyond anything he had expected. Along with that, the heat was overwhelming. Yuki longed for a day off, a chance to rest up. He didn't want to believe that he could be "broken," but Dexter never let him find a moment of peace, never failed to belittle him for whatever he didn't do perfectly. Yuki had been talking for over a year about going off to war and proving himself, but for the first time he was doubting whether he could meet the demands. He had even started to wonder whether Japanese men actually *were* too small, or maybe too soft, to go up against a fierce enemy—big, powerful Germans who were seasoned fighters.

CHAPTER 6

One night, about three weeks into their training, and after a day that left the men in Second Platoon exhausted, they all returned to their barracks, showered, then dropped onto their cots. Some of the men fell asleep, but Yuki noticed more of them staring at the ceiling, as though they were too depleted even to settle down and rest.

"Can we do this?"

Yuki didn't answer for a moment, but he turned his head enough to look at Shig, who was lying on the next cot. "What choice do we have?"

There was no answer to the question. The two just lay there for a time. Yuki felt himself reaching some sort of low point of discouragement. He thought of his mother, his family. He longed to see them. And he let an image come into his head: cute little Keiko in her red dress, standing straight, her feet together, giving him a quick wave.

And then Billy Yamada was leaning over him, between his cot and Shig's. "We're doing better," he said, rather forcefully. "We made our march faster today, and not many broke down before we got to the end of it."

Yuki had no idea what to say.

Yamada was no taller than Yuki, but he was muscular. He was a strawberry farmer from the state of Washington, and he'd been an athlete in high school, a halfback on his football team and a guard in basketball. He didn't brag about any of that, but men from Washington said he was a big name in the Northwest, and he had been offered a sports scholarship to the University of Washington. All the same, he had been bused off with all the other AJA in the area, and stuck in the Minidoka internment camp in Idaho. He had missed his chance to start college. When Yuki had asked him why he had volunteered for the army, he'd merely said, "I wanted to do *something*."

Yamada wasn't a guy who had all that much to say, so it was surprising to Yuki that he was looking rather fierce right now. "Let's quit feeling sorry for ourselves," he said. "We can do anything any other soldier can do."

Yuki liked hearing that. He sat up. "You're right," he said. "It's what I've always said."

By now Yamada was looking at Shig. "I'll put our fire

team up against any team at this camp. It doesn't matter how big you are, Omura. Quit worrying about that."

Billy turned and looked at Makota Okida, a Hawaiian soldier whose cot was foot to foot with Yuki's. Okida was sound asleep, his arms spread out on both sides of his cot, hanging down, and his mouth wide open. "Hey, Oki!" Yamada called out. When Okida didn't respond, he stepped closer. "Oki, wake up."

Okida's mouth closed, and then after a second or two, his eyes opened. "Wha' you say?"

"We're the best fire team on this base. You got that?"

Okida stared at him for a moment, as though the words hadn't quite sunk in yet. But finally he said, "Sho' thing, Billy. We got too many katonks. Thass all."

Yuki laughed, and then so did Shig. There were only four men on the team, three of them mainlanders. Billy grinned and said, "We have too many buddhaheads, if you ask me."

Okida began to smile, and then he broke into a long, deep laugh.

Yuki felt renewed. Like most men in an infantry platoon, the four were riflemen, and they were a fire team—one of two fire teams in the second squad. The four had trained together constantly, and Yuki felt a bond with them. He knew he would depend on them if they ever got to the war. Billy Yamada was only a year older than Yuki, but he was a natural leader, someone to trust.

"Okay," Yuki said, "let's not let anything stop us—not even Sergeant Dexter."

Oki had shut his eyes again, but he said in his mellow voice, "He jussa white guy from da mainland. He don know no betta."

"He's trying to make men out of us," Billy said. "I don't like the way he goes about it, but I gotta say, we're tougher than we were a month ago."

"I tough 'nough," Oki said. "You katonks betta do betta." He laid his arm across his eyes, still smiling, but after a few seconds he was breathing deeply, asleep again.

Yuki glanced at Shig, and they nodded to each other. Yuki felt a little better, and he thought Shig did too.

But life didn't get easier. In the fifth week, the recruits were introduced to an obstacle course. They had to crawl on their stomachs with live ammunition firing over their heads, jump across muddy ditches, climb ropes, and scale a high wall. This last was hard enough for anyone to do, but for such small men, the wall was a trial. They leaped and grabbed at the top to swing themselves up and over, but most failed and then had to take second and third runs at it—and a lot of them still failed. Poor Shig was entirely too short. Dexter swore at him, used filthy language, and then shouted, "You're a pygmy, Omura. You've got no place in this man's army. I'm sending you home to your mama."

This was the kind of stuff Shig had been hearing

all his life. Yuki knew how hard he took such things. Shig ran at the wall for the fourth time, leaped and hit his knee hard, then grabbed at the top of the wall but didn't come close to reaching it. When he dropped onto the dirt, he stayed down for a moment. Yuki was afraid he had broken his kneecap. But he got himself up and limped back to make another try. Dexter yelled at him, "Stop, Omura! Let the others go on by. You're holding everyone up."

Yuki made it over the wall on his second try, and then he pushed himself through the rest of the course. At the end he dropped to the ground with the other recruits, all of them out of breath and exhausted. He kept watching for Shig, who took quite a while to catch up. He was clearly out of gas when he finally made it to the finish line. He dropped on the ground and clutched the knee he had injured.

"Are you okay?" Yuki asked, still gasping for breath himself.

Shig lay there on the hard red clay, drawing in all the air he could. He didn't try to speak for some time, but eventually he said, "I can't get over that wall. There's no way I ever will."

"They said we have to make it."

"I know. Dexter told me. I have to make it or I wash out."

"When? Next time?"

"I don't know. That's all he said."

"We'll figure it out," Yuki said. "We'll get you over that thing some way."

But it didn't happen the next day or the day after that. And the more Shig tried, the more he battered his hands and knees. Then one day in the mess hall, Sergeant Matsumoto showed up at their table just as they were about to head back to the training ground. "Omura, you have to run up the wall," he said. "They won't tell you that. They want you to figure it out. But it's the only way someone your size can do it."

Shig was staring at the sergeant. "How did you know that I couldn't do it?"

"Never mind. It doesn't matter how I know. Run at the wall and then keep right on running. It might take you three steps before you can jump up and grab the top."

"I don't think I can do that. How do you—"

"Just do it. It works. Big guys can't do it that way, but you're quick, and your short legs are actually an advantage."

Yuki could see the doubt in Shig's eyes. He had seen the same thing back on the baseball diamond when Shig made errors. Shig never wanted to call attention to himself, never wanted people to think he couldn't do as well as anyone else. If he dropped a ground ball or made a bad throw, he usually messed up again, the doubt seeming to get into his head. "Shig, don't worry," Yuki told him. "Think how quick you are. Just show the big guys what you can do. We'll go out there tonight and you can try it—when no one else is around."

"We're not allowed to be out on the course at night."

"I don't care. We'll do it. We'll figure it out."

So at the end of the day, when Yuki and Shig hardly felt like taking another step, they slipped out of their hut-ment as the sun was almost gone, and Shig tried what Sergeant Matsumoto had told him. His knee was still bothering him, and his first few tries didn't go well, but Yuki tried it himself, got the idea, and then showed Shig not to leap too high, but to hit the wall running.

"You know what the buddhaheads say: 'Go for broke,'" Yuki told Shig. The Hawaiian soldiers loved to play dice, and when they put every cent they had on the line, that's what they called it: going for broke.

Shig didn't answer, just nodded. And he still didn't make it on the next try. But he came close, and Yuki could see that he was getting the idea. "Okay, that's enough for tonight," he told Shig. "You're too tired. But you'll make it tomorrow, no question."

When the time came for the obstacle course the next day, Yuki made sure that Shig was ahead of him. Shig didn't make it on the first try, but his hand did touch the top, and he clearly had the technique figured out. He dropped well back and ran again, this time not jumping so high but keeping his legs pumping. He clambered up the wall and grabbed the top, then with a mighty pull, made it over.

A lot of men cheered for him, and several others made it over the wall for the first time that day. It seemed to Yuki that the *Nisei* soldiers were beginning to believe in themselves—and each other. He felt it in himself.

New recruits received no days of leave for the first six weeks, but when they finally got a pass to get off the base for a day, Yuki and Shig walked into Hattiesburg. They ran into Sergeant Matsumoto, and he told them about a good little diner, so they walked there with him. Yuki loved the place. It was like the diners where he had eaten in California. He ordered a hamburger and french fries and a chocolate malt. A jukebox was playing songs like "For Me and My Gal" and "Don't Get Around Much Anymore." It all seemed just a little too good to be true.

A family—a husband and wife, an older son, and a teenage daughter—came into the diner and sat down at the next table. Yuki knew farmers when he saw them, and he liked the down-home look of these people. He nodded and smiled. But he heard the young man whisper to his dad. The only words he heard clearly were "those Japs." And the father said something like "more and more of them."

Something about exerting himself in training, being part of the war effort, had made Yuki feel that he no longer had to deal with the old prejudices. He looked at Sergeant Matsumoto, who nodded and said softly, "I know. I heard it. Don't let it bother you."

The three talked about their training, laughed about Shig having become the star of the recruits by showing the others how to climb the wall.

"Thanks for letting me in on the secret," Shig told the sergeant.

"That's all right. I'm not supposed to help you out, but to tell the truth, I get tired of how the army does things. I don't think the way most NCOs do. I only joined the army because I had a college degree and couldn't find a job. I thought the military would let me use my education and work as an engineer. I never expected to lead anyone into battle."

"So what do you want to do when the war's finally over?" Yuki asked.

"First, we gotta be sure we win."

"We will. But then what?"

"I don't know. I don't require much to be happy. I'd like to have a family, a nice little house, books to read, some good music to listen to. That would be enough for me."

"Where do you want to live? In Hawaii?"

"Probably. I have four pretty sisters, and they're all still there. So are my parents. I'd like to be close to them. But a lot of it depends on finding a job."

"Things will be different when we come home, don't you think, Sergeant?"

"You can call me Mat when we're away from the base. That's what most people call me." He leaned back in his chair. "I hope you're right, Yuki. But I don't ever expect people to treat me like I'm just another guy. I'm caught more in the middle than you two are, with parents of different races. But that's another reason to go back to Hawaii. It's less of a problem over there."

"So what about these sisters of yours?" Shig asked Mat. "Just *how* pretty are they?"

This was something new for Shig, and it surprised Yuki. Shig seemed to have gained a little confidence lately. Maybe it was getting over that wall—and having people notice him for it.

"They're all beautiful, if you ask me," Mat said, "and one is about your age. She's the youngest. The other three are older than I am."

"How tall is the young one?" Shig asked with a smile.

"I'd say she's about your size. You're six feet tall, aren't you?"

"More or less."

"That's what I thought. I'll tell you this much. She's as nice a person as I know, and she'd like you. You're a good guy, Shig. And that's what matters to her."

"Well, maybe I'll look her up after the war. I've always wanted to see Hawaii."

"I'll fix you up with a date," Mat said. "Of course, she's studying to be a nurse. You never know; she might meet some wounded soldier by then and nurse him right into holy matrimony."

Shig nodded and said, "A lot of the girls back home are going to be taken by the time we get back."

"It'll even out," Mat said. "A lot of us won't make it home."

Maybe he had meant this to be a joke, but it didn't feel that way. Shig nodded and so did Yuki. Yuki had begun to think about that possibility lately. In the obstacle course, when bullets were buzzing over his head, the chance of getting hit by one in a real battle seemed anything but remote. What he wondered sometimes was what it would be like to have a bullet rip into his body.

"You know what I'd feel worst about if I didn't make it back?" Mat asked.

"What?"

"Never seeing my sisters again. My big sisters all babied me when I was growing up, and my little sister—Kimoka, or just Kimi—she was my best friend until I went off to college. I haven't seen her much in recent years, and I miss her."

"Do you believe in heaven?" Shig asked. And Yuki knew what he was thinking—another way to see her.

Mat looked at Shig for a long time, and then he finally said, "I don't know. I've always believed in the idea of it.

But when I think about getting shot, all that comes to mind is darkness. Just the end of everything."

Yuki wasn't sure what he thought about that. He had worried more about pain than he had about darkness. He wondered which was worse. But he didn't want to continue this conversation. "We're all coming back," he said. "We'll take care of each other."

They all nodded, all agreed.

When the three were finished with their meal, they got their checks and then stood up to walk to the cashier counter. On a sudden impulse, Yuki stepped to the next table where the family was sitting.

"Hello there," he said. "We're in basic training out at the base." He smiled. "We don't like the training much, but we appreciate you local people putting up with us while we're here."

The three who could see Yuki looked up, obviously surprised. The mother twisted around to see who was speaking. No one could come up with a word to say.

"Are you farmers?" Yuki asked.

The man nodded. He was a thin man, all bone, like so many men who had worked the earth all their lives. His face was burned from the sun, but his forehead was ivory white.

"I grew up on a farm in California," Yuki continued. "We raised produce and sold it from a road stand near our farm. I know what it's like to make a living from the land."

The man nodded again. The young man's eyes had drifted down to the checkered oilcloth on the table.

"We're just glad we can fight for our country," Yuki said. He looked at the young man, who had to be close to draft age. "I guess you'll be enlisting before long yourself."

The boy raised his head. "Well . . . I . . . cain't. I won't be able to."

"That's too bad. Those of us training now are all Japanese Americans, as you probably know. We love our country, the same as all of you, and we're glad we can do our part."

The older man nodded one more time but with no more conviction than before.

"My name is Yukus Nakahara. I'm glad to meet you. We hope we won't be too much bother to you around here. But thanks for welcoming us." He stuck his hand out, held it in front of the young man. A second or two passed, and then his hand came up. He shook Yuki's hand, not exactly firmly, and then Yuki offered his hand to the father, who gave him a better handshake.

Yuki nodded to the mother and sister and said, "Have a nice day."

He had already turned away from the table when the older man said, with a deeply southern accent, "Good luck to yuh, young man."

Yuki turned back and smiled. "Thanks," he said. "It's great to have your support."

CHAPTER 7

November 1943–June 1944

There were times when Yuki seriously thought he would never leave Camp Shelby. Basic training gave way to war games, and these dragged on all winter. The rumor Yuki heard was that American generals were hesitating to employ the 442nd troops in actual battle. By the spring of 1944, however, the 100th Infantry Battalion was making a name for itself fighting in Italy. These were *Nisei* soldiers from Hawaii who had quickly become known as the "Purple Heart Battalion" because of their bravery and the unit's many casualties.

The men of the Four-Four-Two hoped that the 100th Battalion had proved the capability of AJA soldiers—but no orders came and the training continued. Yuki found himself frustrated and angry. The last thing he wanted to do was to spend the entire war training in Mississippi.

Then in March the order finally came, and in April the Second and Third Battalions of the 442nd were transported to Virginia and shipped across the ocean from there. All his life Yuki had longed to see the world, but tossing on the ocean was not quite the pleasure he had expected. He and Shig were both sick for a few days before they became accustomed to the motion. After that, it was the tedium that bothered them, as the ship convoy zigged and zagged to avoid detection by German U-boats. Yuki felt the distance, too, as the ship took him farther and farther from everything he had always known. What lay ahead was "the war," which had always been a vague sort of concept, not a reality. He wondered what actual battle would be like. He never told Shig, or anyone else, but he was becoming increasingly worried that he wouldn't be as brave as he wanted to be.

More than three thousand *Nisei* soldiers eventually arrived in Naples, Italy, where they were attached to the army's Thirty-Fourth Infantry Division, which was made up of more than ten thousand white soldiers. Whites and *Nisei* would not be integrated into the same units, but they would fight in the same campaigns and support one another.

After a few days of specialized training, the men of the 442nd were transported by ship and truck northward along the coast of Italy. They marched the last miles, until they approached the German line of defense in the central part of the peninsula. Yuki felt the tension as the men neared the battlefront. They still joked—some even bragged—but not with the ease he had seen before.

Italy had entered the war as one of the three Axis powers, along with Germany and Japan, but almost a year earlier Italian forces had been overpowered by Allied troops—Americans, British, Canadians, and others—and had surrendered. Still, the central and northern parts of Italy were occupied by German troops. Yuki had read about the war in Italy in newspapers, listened to the talk on board the ship, and received briefings from his officers. What he understood was that the Allies were steadily pushing toward Germany. Russia was attacking Germany from the east, and in recent days a huge Allied force had landed on the coast of France in what was being called the "D-Day" invasion. Germany was now being pressured from all directions, but its soldiers were fighting desperately, with no sign of capitulation. The campaign through Italy was proving difficult, and as Allied troops pressed higher into the mountains, the fight was becoming ever more bloody.

By late June, the Four-Four-Two was ready to enter the action. Yuki had trouble sleeping that last night before their first attack. He had heard the sound of artillery by then, miles away, and he had even glimpsed men in bandages being trucked back from the front. The war was finally turning into reality, but it was still hard to imagine

that he might fire his rifle at the enemy in the morning—
and be fired upon.

He eventually drifted into a sort of half sleep, shortly
before he heard the voice of Fred Koba, his platoon sergeant, outside his tent. "Roll out, men. Get something to
eat. We're moving out in an hour."

Sergeant Koba was an experienced military man, having served in the army for many years before the war. He
was no bigger than Yuki, and he was not forceful or loud,
but he knew the men in the platoon from their training
back in Mississippi. He could be stern, but there was also
a fatherly quality about him. He was not in charge of the
platoon, but Yuki had noticed that Lieutenant Freeman,
the platoon leader, depended on Sergeant Koba as more
than an assistant. Everyone trusted that it was Koba who
would know what to do when the action started.

The men got ready quickly. Yuki had the feeling that
no one had slept well. The battalion support unit had
already prepared a hot breakfast, but Yuki couldn't face
the powdered eggs and Spam. He ended up eating only a
little toast with a cup of coffee.

Lieutenant Freeman talked to the men briefly. "Fox
Company will move out first," he told them. "E Company
will be on our right flank, and G Company in a support
position. Remember your training. Follow commands."

The men in Second Platoon liked the lieutenant. Yuki
knew that they all connected better to Sergeant Koba

than to him, but Lieutenant Freeman was one white officer who respected his AJA soldiers. He was a lanky guy, over six feet tall, slim, and light haired. One of the men had joked that he was like a giraffe in a herd of ponies, but Yuki liked that he wasn't overly impressed with himself. He wasn't a lot older than most of the men he was leading, but it seemed to Yuki that he was in control of himself, that he wouldn't lose his head when bullets started to fly.

Yuki tried to breathe in some of that self-confidence, but his hands were shaking so badly that he had to tuck his thumbs into the straps on his backpack to keep them still. As daylight began to break, the troops moved out, and it felt better to get going. Yuki was careful, watchful, and after a mile or so of walking, he had calmed down a bit. The area was flat, all open fields and pastures. There was nowhere for enemy soldiers to hide except in a few scattered farmhouses, but Yuki wondered what sort of artillery might be taking aim from the distant hilltops in front of them. Still, by ten in the morning—ten hundred hours, as the military called it—he had seen no sign of Germans. The company had passed some burned-out Sherman tanks and German *Panzer* tanks, and that had reminded Yuki that the war really was close, but the day was clear, birds were flying about, and a few clouds were scattered across a blue sky. It was hard to believe that a war was waiting up ahead.

Shig had hardly spoken a word all morning. Yuki

finally said to him, "If we're going to engage the Germans, I'm thinking it's going to be in those hills we're coming to. That's where they've probably set up their MLR." That MLR—main line of resistance—was what the company had been ordered to locate. It was the front line, where the battle would begin.

Shig nodded.

"We'll be all right."

"Yeah. Sure." But Yuki could see behind Shig's little round eyeglasses that his eyes were tight and a little too focused. He finally had a uniform that fit him, and he had shown himself to be as "big" as any of the men when it came to carrying out training drills, but he was stiff this morning, no doubt scared the same as Yuki.

Still, he and Yuki marched steadily ahead with the others. All morning Yuki had been hearing the growl of artillery fire, but the sound was increasing, sharpening, and the hills were no longer far off.

Sergeant Koba worked his way down the line and spoke to the squad leaders. Yuki heard him tell Sergeant Oshira, Yuki and Shig's squad leader, "If we get fired on, keep your men together. Listen for the lieutenant's command."

Sergeant Oshira led two fire teams in his squad, eight men, all of whom had become close friends in the last year. "Sarge," as the men usually called Oshira, was Hawaiian, but like Koba, he had been in the army before the war broke out, and he used Pidgin only when he joked with the buddhaheads. He was a small man, slightly built, but he was wiry. Once, in training, a recruit had lost his temper and challenged him. Sarge had used a judo move and the young soldier had landed on his back, stunned.

Mat Matsumoto was the leader of another eight-man squad. He was friendly with Yuki and Shig, but he was not so casual as he had been back at Shelby. Mat had told Yuki and Shig the night before, "Everyone tells me that the first time in battle is the most dangerous—since new troops don't know how to look out for themselves yet. Don't take any chances. Just follow what your leaders tell you."

Yuki was walking rather easily now, not observing everything as carefully as he had early that morning, but then his eye caught a motion on the ridge of a low hill a few hundred yards ahead. There was a farmhouse on the hill, and Yuki thought a farmer must be driving about on his tractor. But suddenly a muzzle protruded from behind the house, and then a tank swung into view. "Tank!" someone shouted, and everyone halted. They all stood as though locked in place. There was a bright flash from the muzzle, a puff of smoke, followed by a deep thump. Yuki knew a shell was on its way, even heard the whistling sound, but his brain didn't let the danger register. Not two seconds later, there was a huge explosion among the men up ahead. Dirt and debris flew in all directions and someone screamed in pain.

The men scattered off the road. Some clambered up

an incline on the right side; others flung themselves into a little drop-off to the left.

Yuki dove toward the ditch and flattened himself in the long grass just as another crash shook the ground. He heard more screams. Someone rolled over him, as more men tumbled down the hill. Yuki pressed his body against the earth. Another high-pitched buzz was sounding. He gripped his hands over his helmet, pulled the liner tight against his head as the explosion shook his body and sucked the air from his lungs.

Nothing followed for a few seconds, and Yuki raised his head just enough to see where Sergeant Oshira might be. He had no idea what he should do next. There was nowhere to hide and seemingly no way to stop the barrage. The tank could just keep firing until the whole company was wiped out.

And then Yuki saw Johnny Fukumoto—a guy from the heavy weapons squad, but a kid his own age—scrambling onto the road. He knelt down about twenty yards ahead of Yuki and dropped a mortar plate onto the ground. He set up a mortar tube quickly, and then he looked through the sight and twisted a knob. He needed an assistant to load and fire, needed a forward observer to be accurate. Yuki was sure he was going to die out there. But Fukumoto dropped a shell into the tube, ducked, and covered his ears, and Yuki heard the hollow *thunk* as the round fired.

Almost simultaneously, a shell from the German tank struck on the high side of the road. But Fukumoto didn't run for cover. Yuki watched as he loaded and fired a second mortar. At the same time, another shell from the German tank was screaming through the air. The explosion burst directly in front of the mortar tube. Yuki saw Johnny flip into the air, cartwheel, and then slam to the ground. His shoulder collapsed under him and he folded onto his side. He seemed to deflate, lose shape, and he made a wet, sucking sound as he tried to breathe. He grabbed his neck with both hands and blood oozed between his fingers. The gurgling noise—the hoarse, vibrating sound—was sickening. Yuki ducked his head, pulled his helmet tight again. He thought he should help Johnny somehow, but he couldn't move, couldn't get himself to go out on that road.

The gurgling lasted only half a minute, but each gasp was like a knife stab to Yuki. He told himself over and over to get up and help the guy, and he almost did, but the sound gave way to choking and suddenly stopped.

Yuki had always known that friends of his would die.

But he hadn't known.

His brain didn't want to accept the idea. "The tank's moving back," someone shouted. But Yuki still couldn't move.

Sergeant Koba was yelling by then. "Get up! Get going. We've got to get away from this road."

Yuki tried to get up, thought he was about to do it.

But nothing was happening. His body wanted to stay on the ground.

"Charge that farmhouse! Make it up that hill."

Charge *toward* the farmhouse? Yuki had expected a command to fall back. But he heard men scrambling to their feet, glanced up to see them moving, and his muscles finally responded. He got up. He didn't know where Shig was, where his squad was. There was still dust in the air from the explosion, and chaos was all around him—men scattering more than charging. He wasn't sure where the farmhouse was, not even the hill, but he felt men moving around him, stayed with that flow of motion, and before long he could see the hillside.

And then the whistling sound was filling the air again. Yuki dropped onto his chest before the blast hit farther up the hillside. The tank could still fire, or maybe there was another one. And there was something new: popping sounds, in bursts. Machine-gun fire. Yuki flattened himself, clung to his helmet again, expected at any moment to feel pain cut through his body.

"Keep moving! Keep moving!" Sergeant Koba was shouting. "You'll die out here if you don't keep moving."

That made no sense to Yuki. He couldn't stand up with bullets in the air.

But some men were up, and then Shig was next to him.

"Get up, Yuki!" he was yelling. "Get up!"

Another couple of seconds passed. It was just time

enough to think that he couldn't do it. But then he did. He jumped to his feet and charged up the hill. There was one more explosion, and more machine-gun fire—the buzz of bullets in the air. But he kept going, climbing hard. He had lost sight of Shig, didn't know who was next to him, but he kept his eyes on the farmhouse and he kept going.

Up ahead, Yuki saw an explosion, and then two more, and he dropped down again. But he knew at the same moment that these explosions, this debris, had silenced the machine gun. Some of the men in his company had gotten up the hill far enough, must have tossed grenades into the machine-gun emplacement.

From somewhere, Lieutenant Freeman's reedy voice was shouting, "Get to the farmhouse!"

Yuki got up. If he could make it up the hill, hide behind the solid rock of that farmhouse, he would be safe, he thought. He kept running hard, and when he made it to the house, he dropped down next to it, pushed his shoulder against the base of the wall, and then waited to see what would happen next.

"The tank's gone," someone said—someone breathing as hard as he was.

And someone else said, "We got the machine gun."

"We have men down," Sergeant Koba shouted. "We gotta get back to 'em and get 'em off that hill."

Some of the men got up and ran down the hill. Yuki still didn't move.

Shig showed up after a few minutes. He dropped down next to Yuki. "Are you okay?" he asked.

Yuki didn't know. What had come into his head was that he was a coward. He had panicked. He had felt the way he had when he was a little kid and had fallen into an irrigation ditch. He had clung to a tree limb and screamed for his father. And Father had dragged him out. But he hadn't known what to do in that water, couldn't think how to save himself. He had felt the fear like a sickness, like that out-of-control moment when he was about to vomit and his body just did what it wanted to do.

"I couldn't move," Yuki told Shig.

"I know."

"But *you* got up."

"Not at first. Sergeant Oshira grabbed me and pulled me up. I couldn't get myself to do it."

"I didn't know it was like this."

That was all Yuki could say. He felt sure he couldn't face this kind of fear day after day. He couldn't run toward bullets and explosions. He couldn't hear a man drown, breathing in his own blood. He wanted to go home.

He stayed by the wall, and after a time he looked around and saw that a lot of other men were looking the way he must look—their faces dirty and their eyes full of wonder and confusion. Had they fired their rifles? Yuki hadn't fired his. Had they fought the Germans, or had they thought only of saving themselves, the way he had?

Down the hill, medics were taking care of the wounded, and some of the soldiers were carrying limp men—dead men, maybe—back to the bottom of the hill. They were doing what they had to do. Yuki wanted to be part of that, not part of the fear. He spotted Sergeant Oshira and Billy Yamada, his fire team leader, working together to carry a man on a litter. He finally got himself up, but Sergeant Koba said, "That's okay, Nakahara. They've got things handled down there. Stay where you are for now."

After a time, Sergeant Koba stood before the men who had gathered at the farmhouse, maybe three or four dozen of them. But it wasn't a full platoon. It was a mix of men who had charged helter-skelter, having lost all sense of organization. Other groups were scattered in various directions, and a good many had been hit by the shells or the machine-gun fire. "Take a rest," Koba told them. "Drink some water. Sit tight and get some food in you." He didn't sound tough or angry. In fact, he seemed concerned about his men. Yuki knew in an instant that he wanted to be like that, wanted to have that much control, that kind of attitude.

Sergeant Koba walked away, and Yuki pulled his canteen from the pouch on his belt. He took a big drink of the lukewarm water. It tasted bad, but he took three long tugs on it and realized how thirsty he had been. But he couldn't eat, didn't try. He shut his eyes and tried to rest.

What he found, however, was that his head was full of pictures—dirt flying, men scattering, smoke, Fukumoto's body rising, turning over in the air. It seemed to Yuki that an hour or two ago he had been himself and now he was someone else.

No one was talking. Yuki knew the other soldiers were processing their own thoughts—the new pictures they had in their own heads.

Finally, word came from the officers of the company to fall back to an assembly point near a little stream lower in the valley. Once they were there, Lieutenant Freeman gathered all the men in the platoon around him. They had started with four squads, more than thirty men, but it was obvious to Yuki that a good many were missing now. He tried to think who was gone. He could see Corporal Billy Yamada and Shig and Oki. His fire team had survived. Corporal Don Fujii, the other fire team leader in his squad, was sitting on the ground nearby. Fujii was another Hawaiian, a guy who loved to laugh, loved to play dice or poker and bet all he had, but right now he looked solemn.

Next to Fujii were Ted Tanna and Yoshi Higa, members of Fujii's team. They were friends from high school, like Yuki and Shig, both from Portland, Oregon. They had been distance runners in school, and they could march all day without a problem. But they were leaning forward, their elbows on their raised knees. And Yuki realized why.

Shiro Tahara—a boy they called Ty—was not with them. Tahara had been part of their squad since basic training. He was Hawaiian, a college student before he joined up. He came from a big family, talked about his brothers and sisters all the time.

"Where's Ty?" Yuki asked.

When Tanna and Yoshi looked up, Yuki saw the despair in their eyes. "He went down," Yoshi said.

"Dead?"

Yoshi nodded, and then he and Tanna ducked their heads again.

The squad—eight friends—had been together from the beginning, and suddenly, in the first minutes of battle, one of them was gone. It seemed impossible. Yuki ducked his own head.

"The Krauts have fallen back," the lieutenant told the men in the platoon. "This was just an outpost. Their MLR is still up ahead. But we've got to get better organized tomorrow." He stood with his long legs spread wide, and he pulled off his helmet. He ran his fingers over his cropped blond hair. "Our communication system failed. We didn't know where Companies E and G were, and we got out ahead of them. We need to regroup."

He stood for a time, gazed around at the men. He looked as dirty as the others, but he didn't look scared. Yuki was glad for that.

"You fell apart on me, men. You scattered." He let

that sink in, and then he said, "But don't be too hard on yourselves. You were scared to get up and charge that hill, but you did it. And some of you figured out what we had to do. You knocked out the machine gun and saved the rest of us."

"Sergeant Koba did that," someone said.

"Not alone, he didn't." Lieutenant Freeman used his sleeve to wipe the sweat off his face. "You'll do better in coming days. You faced the enemy today. You found out you could keep going no matter how scared you were. That's what you had to learn."

When he paused, the deep silence was obvious.

"What you learned today is that if you go down to the ground in the face of fire, you're just waiting to be killed. When you keep moving ahead, you push the enemy back. It's kill or be killed, and you can't save yourselves if you allow them to shoot at a stationary target."

Yuki had heard all this in training, but he hadn't understood it until now.

"I'm sorry, but we had a lot of our men shot up today, and some were killed. Right now I'm not exactly sure how many. Fukumoto is dead. But I want you to know, he's a hero. I'll put him in for a medal. He saved our platoon—the whole company, really—from getting blown away by that tank. I want you to remember what he did and learn from it. But don't look back too much. You need to concentrate on the next battle, not the last one, and you can't dwell on some of the things you experienced today. You've seen blood now, and you've tasted fear. Use what you've learned and be better soldiers tomorrow."

And then the lieutenant admitted something Yuki hadn't expected. "We officers made mistakes too. We got you into a bad spot, staying on that open road and not knowing where the other companies were. We'll all do better next time."

Maybe so. But Yuki could only think that nothing had been what he had expected. It was hard to imagine that he would feel any better tomorrow.

"Dig in, men," was the lieutenant's last instruction. "We'll camp right here tonight."

CHAPTER 8

Yuki and Shig worked on a foxhole together that evening, but their exhaustion soon won out and they didn't manage to dig very deep. Yuki had always wondered whether he would be able to sleep when he actually reached the battlefront, but he curled up on the hard ground at the bottom of the hole and fell asleep instantly. He didn't wake until early the next morning, when he heard reverberations again—explosions from distant artillery shells.

He stirred then and realized that his muscles were aching—surely from the running and diving to the ground the day before, but also from the cramped position he had been in all night. He was still tired and grimy, but once he got up and ate some canned ham and a couple of hard biscuits from his C-ration packet, he felt a kind of satisfaction that he hadn't expected. The heat hadn't come on yet, and the day seemed pleasant—no matter what had happened the day before. "Hey, Shig," he said. "We made it. We got through our first battle."

Shig took a long look at Yuki. He seemed mystified by Yuki's attitude. "Yeah," he said. "That's what we did. We got through."

"Maybe it gets easier after a while."

"I don't see how, Yuki." Shig was sitting on the edge of the foxhole staring at an open can of ham, as though he were building up his courage to eat it. But then he looked up at Yuki and added, "You always try to make the best of things, and I guess that's good, but I don't want to go through anything like that ever again."

"I'm pretty sure it won't be *every* day. And we won't be quite so scared next time."

Shig continued to look into Yuki's eyes, his own eyes full of questions, but then he ducked his head, stabbed the fork from his mess kit into the ham, and took a bite of it—resolutely, as though this were one more thing that had to be done. Yuki was worried about him. Shig stuck with things, kept trying even when he doubted himself, but Yuki had never seen him this discouraged. Yuki realized that was the main reason he had tried to sound optimistic: to bolster his own confidence, but mostly to raise Shig's spirits.

It struck him now, however, that Lieutenant Freeman's instruction not to look backward was probably right.

What he was fighting back were thoughts of his mother, his family, Keiko. He had vowed to return to them, even bragged that he would. But now, after only one battle, he could see how arrogant he had been. His company had faced one tank and an outpost of soldiers. What would happen when they faced the full wrath of the German forces?

The seven men who were left in Yuki's squad—along with their squad leader, Sergeant Oshira—had all dug in close to one another, and after breakfast they waited for further orders. No one mentioned Tahara, but Yuki knew he was on everyone's mind. Ted Tanna and Yoshi Higa were talkative guys, but they were saying almost nothing today. Yuki heard Sergeant Oshira say, "I should have kept the squad together. But everything went crazy." He wasn't one to express much self-doubt, but Yuki could hear in his voice the sorrow he was feeling.

Before long, Sergeant Koba came by. "Lieutenant Freeman just told me we're sitting tight today," he said. "We won't move out until tomorrow."

"What's going on?" Sergeant Oshira asked.

"They're sending the 100th Battalion forward. They're supposed to sweep around the hill we fought on yesterday and attack the Germans at the MLR." The 100th Battalion had been attached to the 442nd Regimental Combat Team and had taken the place of First Battalion, which had remained at Camp Shelby.

Private Okida had been resting, lying flat on his back, but he sat up now. He hadn't been saying much that morning either, but now he asked, "How come da One Puka Puka go, an' not us? Dey betta'n us?"

Yuki had learned that "puka" actually meant "hole" in Pidgin, but buddhaheads also used it to mean "zero," so the 100th had become "One Puka Puka."

Sergeant Koba smiled a little. He clearly liked Oki. But he wasn't one to joke around. "Yeah, they're better than we are," he said. "Until we improve." He stepped closer to Okida. "Have you got a smoke?"

"Sho, Sergeant. Sit down. Tek a rest."

Koba didn't sit down, but he took the cigarette that Oki handed him. He lit up, blew the smoke out through his nostrils, and said, "Those 100th boys are the best. They fought at Monte Cassino—a mountaintop they had to take from the Germans on their way to Rome. They lost more than half their men, but the Krauts know them, and know how tough they are. That's what we have to do—let the Germans know that when they fight us, they might as well get ready to retreat."

After Sergeant Koba walked away, the men talked about becoming the fighters they needed to be. Sergeant Oshira was more adamant than Koba. "I'm telling you, men, we'll be like that. But we've got to catch on fast. We can't keep taking losses the way we did yesterday."

Yuki looked around, wondered whether the men in

the squad could ever be as fierce as required. Billy Yamada had the guts to be a tough fighter; so did Don Fujii. But Yuki could sense that Tanna and Higa were still as overwhelmed as he and Shig were. And maybe Oki was too mellow. If the squad was going to be what it needed to be, Yuki knew he had to be more like his leaders. He had to show Shig and the others that a young soldier could grow up fast.

As it turned out, the 100th Battalion marched past Yuki's battalion that morning. Yuki saw how confident they looked. They joked a little, the way the buddhaheads usually did, but Yuki could see how resolved they were. They did stop long enough to take a breather, however, and some of the men in the company greeted relatives or friends from Hawaii.

An older guy in the 100th, a first sergeant, spoke to Muki Shimuzu. Muki, the Hawaiian soldier Yuki and Shig had met on their first day at Camp Shelby, was in Mat Matsumoto's squad. "Wha' go down here yestaday?" the first sergeant asked.

Muki shrugged. "I dunno. We mess up."

"We gotta go fix yo mess now," the man said. "You betta do betta—an' fast."

Yuki felt the reproof. He thought of himself the day before, flat on the ground and wanting never to get up. He told himself he would never do that again, no matter what happened to him.

The men rested that day. By evening, word was spreading through the troops that the 100th had attacked the MLR and wiped out the German forces, taking lots of prisoners, destroying equipment, and forcing a retreat.

The Second and Third Battalions marched forward the next morning. They met little resistance. By the following day, however, Yuki could once again hear the sounds of war getting closer. He watched the troop in front of him, saw their watchfulness in surveying their surroundings. They were changed men from the ones who had strolled into battle that first day. They were thinking—and moving—like soldiers.

Another day passed, and another, and still, except for some sporadic fire, the men faced no actual battle, but tension was growing. Yuki knew the quiet couldn't last much longer.

Then on July 4, Second Battalion was ordered to lead the way in taking the high ground at a site the army had designated as Hill 277. Companies E and G were commanded forward, with Yuki's Company F following in reserve. Yuki found himself relieved not to be out in front, but he told himself he wasn't going to fall apart today.

Yuki's platoon, along with all of Fox Company, hunkered down as the advance companies attacked and came under fire. Yuki watched as the troops drove forward to the crest of the hill. The fire didn't seem as heavy as it had been that first day, but he saw medics carrying *Nisei* soldiers on stretchers down the hill—guys with bloody bandages, some shot in the gut or chest, one with his face entirely bandaged. It was chilling to see what bullets or shrapnel could do to men's bodies.

Fox Company moved up when the shooting stopped, and the men in Sergeant Oshira's squad, along with the rest of the platoon, dug in for the night just below the crest of the hill. But the following morning, the entire battalion was ordered to cross over the ridge and attack the next hill, with E Company leading the way. Before F Company moved out to follow, a bombardment opened. Yuki couldn't see the men descending the hill, but the Germans had the high ground on a facing hill, and the sound of artillery and rifle fire from across the valley was thunderous. The dust and smoke rose in a grimy cloud. Mortars and big artillery guns were spreading their destruction everywhere, and machine-gun fire was targeted on the soldiers from all angles. Yuki had gotten to know a lot of the men in E Company, and it made him sick to think that some of them were dying right now, and that he was about to follow them down that hill.

It wasn't long, however, before men began retreating back over the top. Yuki could see them charging toward him, their faces full of terror. Once out of the line of fire of the German guns, they dropped down, gasping, panting. Some of them had been hit and were bleeding. Yuki, Shig, and a lot of F Company men hurried to them to offer what help they could give. Yuki found one man down on his chest with blood pumping from a gash in his leg. "Hang on! I'll get the bleeding stopped!" he shouted to the man, who was moaning and cursing. But a medic arrived and took over, and Yuki was only needed to help carry the soldier to an aid station.

That evening, Sergeant Koba told his men that all four platoon leaders in E Company had been killed or wounded during their attack. It was hard for Yuki to imagine the company going forward with all their experienced leaders wiped out. Some of his new resolve was seeping away. But he also felt something else for the first time: a bitter anger. The first battle had left him scared, but this time he had watched the slaughter and had had the chance to think about what it meant. Those German soldiers were fighting for everything that was wrong. They had probably celebrated as they blasted all his AJA brothers. He wanted some revenge for that. He had talked about Krauts in training, and he opposed everything the Nazis stood for: their hatred of all races other than white, their brutal control and mistreatment of civilians in the countries they had defeated. But all that was an idea, an abstraction. Today, German soldiers had rained down fire on his friends and had ripped their bodies open. He wanted to make them pay for that.

Later that night, Lieutenant Freeman called the platoon together. "All right, men," he said, "Fox Company takes the lead tomorrow. But we won't move off this ridge in the daytime again. Get some rest now because we're moving out in the night—oh two hundred hours."

Two in the morning. It wasn't the early hour that bothered Yuki; it was moving out in the dark. He wondered what would happen if the troops took fire and couldn't see anything.

"G Company is going with us, and we're going to work our way off this hill and swing around to the side of Hill 140. That's the one straight ahead of us where the Germans fired from today. We'll climb that hill and then attack before the sun comes up. We've got to bust them off the high ground. If we do this right, we won't take many casualties. Move in silence, and then, when we attack, go after the Germans with everything you've got. Attack like samurai." He stopped and nodded, and Yuki liked that he knew about those ancient warriors. "First Platoon will make the initial charge, and they're going to fix their bayonets in case they catch men still sacked out. If we pull this off, the enemy will be rousted out of their sleep and won't put up much resistance."

Yuki wondered whether two companies of fighters—around two hundred men—could move that quietly and catch seasoned troops off guard in the night. But he reminded himself not to think too much, just to do what he had to do. He tried to laugh when he told Oki, "Don't play your ukulele when we're sneaking up that mountain."

"I won't. But I sing 'Aloha Oi' so they know the buddhaheads comin'. Dey know we *warriors*—like lutenan' say."

The men in Yuki's squad laughed a little, but nervously, and then they settled down in their foxholes and tried to sleep. At 0130, Sergeant Koba awakened the platoon. Those who weren't too nervous managed to eat a little, but Yuki couldn't stand to look at food. He merely got his pack and rifle ready, and then lined up when Sergeant Oshira called his squad together with the rest of the platoon. When the men moved out, they were in double columns, but in the dark, each concentrated on staying close to the backpack in front of him.

The pace was slow and careful, but the troops descended the hill in less than half an hour, and then they took about that long again to swing to the east of Hill 140. They worked their way up for a time, then made a switchback and continued the slow climb. No one spoke, but Yuki could hear the steps, the slips, equipment and weapons clicking and rattling as they walked. He felt sure they would be heard before much longer, and then they would have to make an all-out charge the rest of the way.

The column stopped, and everyone paused. Yuki assumed that the soldiers in First Platoon were fixing their bayonets and waiting for the signal to attack. But then the column moved again, and Lieutenant Freeman directed his soldiers to slip in behind the men of First Platoon, who had fanned out, prepared to start their assault. Yuki could see the silhouettes of the soldiers in front. They were hunched, ready, their rifles at their hips. He could hear his own heart pounding in his ears.

First Platoon set out, not running, but walking hard. Less than a minute went by before Yuki's platoon lined up and headed out on an angle to the left. But they had not gone far before he heard the first report of a German machine pistol, and then the sound of American M1 rifles.

"Let's go," Sergeant Koba called out, and his platoon charged straight up the hill. Yuki heard bullets buzzing in the air and saw bright tracer bullets flying overhead, but the Germans were firing at sounds, not soldiers, and they were aiming too high.

Then Yuki saw flashes of gunfire and he knew that a German machine-gun emplacement was now in operation off to their left, maybe a hundred yards up the hill. He could see Sergeant Oshira moving next to him, and he knew Billy Yamada was on his other side, with Shig and Oki farther to the right. But they were too close to each other. They could all go down if a mortar struck in the middle of them. Sergeant Oshira was obviously thinking the same thing. "Spread out!" he yelled. But just as the men did so, the machine-gun bullets started striking the ground ahead of them.

Yuki fought the desire to veer away or to hit the ground. Lieutenant Freeman had told them that to drop down was only to wait to get hit, so he kept going even as bullets whooshed through the air, making a sharp cracking noise as they passed him.

Sergeant Oshira yelled, "Yamada, take your fire team and go after that machine gun!"

"Let's go!" Yamada shouted, and Yuki chased after him. He could hear Shig and Oki running with him.

"Cover me!" Corporal Yamada yelled.

Yuki understood. He slowed a little, took aim, and shot directly at the muzzle fire of the machine gun. It seemed wrong to slow down, to stand erect before the gunfire. What he wanted to do was to get far away from that machine gun. But he and Shig and Oki were all shooting now, and the machine-gun fire had become sporadic.

But as the bullets let up, mortar fire began to hit the hill. Explosions were going off everywhere. In one flash of light, Yuki saw a *Nisei* soldier get blown off his feet, his arms flailing, his rifle flying from his grip.

Everything was chaos, and Yuki felt something close to panic again. But he continued to fire and to work his way forward. Halfway across the open area in front of him, he found that he had used up a clip of ammo. He grabbed for a new clip, jerked it from his belt, and stopped long enough to click it into place. At the same time, an explosion burst at the spot where the muzzle of the machine gun had been flashing. Someone had thrown a hand grenade into the machine-gun nest.

Yuki ran toward the emplacement. He had to make sure no Germans had survived to start firing again. A mortar shell struck behind him, and the explosion illuminated everything for a moment. Yuki saw a silhouette: a German with his distinctive helmet, the rim turned upward. He aimed and fired, but the light was already gone and he had no idea whether he had hit the man.

Fire from that emplacement had stopped entirely, and another machine gun, off to the right, had also gone silent. More Americans were making it to the ridge. Mortar shells were still dropping onto the hill, but most of the fire was hitting behind the *Nisei* troops now. The Germans were probably trying to avoid hitting their own men.

Yuki was not quite sure what to do, but he wanted to find the men in his squad, so he ran on to the spot where the machine gun had been firing.

"We got 'em all," Corporal Yamada said between gasps.

Sergeant Oshira was also there. "Stay here," he barked. "We're supposed to hold this ridge."

"Where's Shig?" Yuki asked.

"Right here." Shig was running toward Yuki, apparently unhurt.

Shells were still exploding on the lower part of the hillside, but the battle seemed over. The Germans were retreating down the opposite side of Hill 140. The Four-Four-Two had completed its objective, won the battle.

Yuki sat down, realized how hard he was breathing,

how crazily his heart was pounding. But he was relieved, even a little proud of himself.

"We pushed the Germans off the hill," Shig said. Yuki heard the satisfaction in his voice.

"Maybe. Maybe not," Sergeant Oshira said. "Just stay ready. We'll see what the lieutenant tells us to do."

But time passed, and when Lieutenant Freeman did reach the men, he told them, "We're staying put for now. Rest up a little and get some food in you. Then dig in."

Yuki was still not ready to eat, so he decided to start digging. He was glad to have something to do. He and Shig went to work shoveling the hard earth. It was almost morning now and exhaustion was setting in, but Yuki knew he was too nervous to sleep.

After an hour or so, the digging got easier and Yuki and Shig were able to get fairly deep into the ground. The sun began to create a line of light across the horizon, and then the whole sky lightened. Yuki waited until he could see quite well, and then he did what he had been wanting to do. He looked over the pile of rocks that had guarded the machine-gun emplacement. The gun was on its side, a German soldier draped over the top of it. Another man was flat on his back, blood running from his mouth and nose. A third man was off to the side in the spot where Yuki had seen the silhouette. That man was down too, but Yuki couldn't see anything wrong with him. He was lying on his side like a child taking a nap, his legs pulled up toward his chest. Yuki stepped over the rocks and took a closer look. When he saw the soldier's face, he realized it was the face of a boy, not a man. The soldier looked no more than fourteen or fifteen.

Blood had pooled under the boy's head. Yuki couldn't see where the bullet had hit him, but he didn't want to see. He stepped back, shut his eyes. Earlier, he had felt some satisfaction for a moment. He had made a great shot; he had taken out an enemy. But the soldier didn't look like a Nazi, like the brutal Krauts he had always imagined. He was a kid. He should have been home playing soccer with his friends, or sitting in a schoolroom. And he was not just young; he was . . . a person. Or at least he had been.

A question came to mind. Yuki stepped away, didn't ask it. He tried to think of anything else. He talked to the other men, looked down the hill to see how many of his own brothers might have gone down. He wanted his company's casualties to make him mad again, make him feel justified.

But the question was still hovering, too close to ignore: Who was the boy?

And another: When would his family find out that he was dead?

108

CHAPTER 9

After the shelling had stopped, the hillside had become eerily still. But Yuki heard birds singing, as though they were enjoying the rising sun in spite of the turmoil that must have shaken them in the night. There were no tall trees on Hill 140, only pockets of brush and grass, but everything was now scarred with craters, especially farther down the hill. When a ground squirrel ran to the edge of a patch of grass and poked its nose out, Yuki wondered what the poor thing had done while the shells had been falling.

Shig was also watching the squirrel. "The world keeps going, no matter what we do to it," he said.

It was a strange thought to Yuki. It was not just the birds and squirrels who were going about their day. His mother was too, and she had no idea what Yuki had seen in the last couple of weeks. Keiko was going to school, doing her homework, probably dancing on Saturday nights. He had written to his family and to Keiko after arriving in Italy, but no mail had caught up to him yet. He wanted so much to hear from them, to know that the home front was still there, that in some spot in the world no bullets were violating summer days.

"We need to be more like Oki," Yuki said. "He doesn't let anything bother him."

Oki was lying on the ground with his backpack under his head. He was breathing deeply, seemingly asleep. Without opening his eyes, he said, "You got dat wrong. Army food make me sick. Dat bodder me."

Billy Yamada laughed with Yuki and Shig. But Yuki saw something in the men's eyes—and in the eyes of all the other men around him. They were tired, no doubt, and relieved that the battle had ended well, but there was a kind of detachment in their faces, in the way they sat and stared. They had heard bullets burrow through the air, pass over their heads, and now it was starkly clear how much luck it took to get through a battle. Their numbers were smaller again, but Yuki didn't want to think who was missing.

Shig looked especially weary. "Are you okay?" Yuki asked him.

"Sure."

"No, really. Are you?"

Shig raised his head, looked at Yuki straight on, but

his eyes still seemed distant. "I did better this time," he said.

"Maybe we're getting used to things—at least a little."

"I don't want to get used to it," Shig said. "I don't like what we're doing."

Yuki understood. It was what he was feeling too. But he was pretty sure he had even more on his mind than Shig did. He didn't tell Shig that he had killed a boy, that the boy was curled up on his side, not far away. Who could get used to that?

Suddenly Yuki didn't want to sit still, didn't want to think. He wondered whether he could find the soldier who had been knocked off his feet during the charge up the hill. Someone had probably helped him by now, but he wanted to be sure. So he got up and walked down the hill, but in the daylight he couldn't figure out where things had happened. As he was returning to the top of the hill, he saw a man on the ground and a medic on his knees, leaning over him. And then he realized it was Corporal Fujii. Yuki could see a crater where an artillery shell had exploded close to him, saw that shrapnel had torn up his leg and hip and mangled one of his hands. His jaw was also bandaged.

Fujii had obviously received a shot of morphine and was lying still now; the medic was preparing him to be moved. "Is he going to be okay?" Yuki asked.

"I don't think he'll make it," the medic whispered.

"It's probably better if he doesn't. His jaw was almost torn off. I don't see how the docs can put him back together."

Yuki looked away, took a long breath. He listened for the birds, watched some long grass riffle as a breeze came up. Without responding to the medic, he walked back to his squad.

Yuki didn't want to talk about Fujii, but Shig had begun to wonder what had happened to him, and he asked whether Yuki had seen him. "Yeah. I saw him. He's hurt bad" was all Yuki could manage to say.

"We gotta get even with some Krauts for that one," Sergeant Oshira said.

"That's right," Yuki said. But the sergeant had sounded brash, and Yuki couldn't match his tone. A picture was back in his head: the German boy at the gun emplacement, one arm bent at the elbow, his hand almost touching his cheek—as though his last act had been to reach for the place where the bullet had struck. His cheek had been smooth, like a baby's, the boy still too young to shave.

Yuki decided to deepen his foxhole. He needed to do something. He also knew this calm couldn't last much longer. There were still German guns in the area. Artillery fire would surely start again.

Shig finally protested that Yuki was making the hole so deep that he wouldn't be able to climb out. That was an exaggeration, but Yuki got the point: It was deep enough. So he climbed out and looked around. He thought he might help someone else dig. He had noticed Mat Matsumoto digging a foxhole not too far away. Yuki walked over to see how his friend was doing. Mat was sitting with his legs dangling into his foxhole. "Do you think that's deep enough?" he asked Yuki.

"I don't know. I feel like I want to dig to the center of the earth before the Germans start shooting their eighty-eights at us."

"They will, too. They'll want this hill back."

"Why does this hill matter more than any of the others?"

"It's the highest ground around here, and it's strategic. The road down below is the only one big enough for supply trucks to use. We can't keep our push going unless we hold this ground."

"How do you know all that? No one ever tells me anything except 'Stop here and dig in again.'"

"I heard the lieutenant talking to Sergeant Koba. They were looking at a map and talking about the road. But anything Lieutenant Freeman knows, he's getting from the company command post."

"Where is the CP anyway?"

"They're setting it up down off the ridge." Mat laughed. "I guess the captain figures we make better cannon fodder than he does."

Yuki nodded, wished he could think of something to say that sounded as knowing and ironic. But Mat looked as detached as the other men, and his voice had lost some of its life, as though it took all his concentration just to carry on a conversation.

"How did we do this time?" Yuki asked him.

"A lot better." Mat looked at the shovel in his hands, then looked down into the foxhole. His partner, a guy named Del Hirinaka, was lying on a patch of grass nearby, his helmet pulled over his eyes.

Yuki knew the men had performed better this time and that he had done better himself, but he also knew how spent he was, and a loud, persistent ringing was filling his ears. Something in him kept saying, "I've done this. I passed a test last night. But I can't do it again today and then again tomorrow." He wanted to cling to all the resolutions he had made the last couple of days, but for now, he was just too deflated.

He also wondered whether anyone was going to get rid of the German bodies. Would someone bury them? Or would that boy be left to rot where he was?

Yuki hadn't planned to talk about the German boy, but suddenly he found himself saying, "I killed someone last night, Mat. I saw him in a flash of light, and I shot him."

Mat looked up, seemed to recognize what Yuki was feeling, but he only nodded.

"I had a chance to look at him. He was just a young boy."

"That's what's happening now. The Germans have

been fighting this war a long time and they've taken a beating from the Russians on the eastern front. They're forcing boys thirteen and fourteen into the military. They fill them with propaganda in Hitler Youth and then they send them out to kill for the fatherland."

"He just looked like, I don't know, a nice kid."

"Don't talk about it. It just makes things worse."

"I know. But he's right there, on the other side of those rocks." Yuki's voice had begun to shake. He knew he had to stop talking.

"You didn't think up this war, Yuki. We're just doing what we have to do. We can't dwell on stuff like that."

Yuki nodded. He had to let it go. He understood that.

And then he heard that shrill sound in the air again. Two, three, all at once.

"Incoming!" someone yelled, and for a second Yuki forgot to run. The first shell struck beyond the troops, raising a cascade of black earth. By then Yuki was moving. He ran to his foxhole, didn't bother to look in, just jumped, and came down with one foot on Shig's hip. But he didn't take time to apologize; he merely curled up next to Shig, pulled his helmet on tight, and then held onto it as the shells fell in a wild barrage, one explosion blending with another, the ground seeming to roll like waves. One shell struck close, and Yuki felt the compression actually lift him off the ground. Dirt rained into the hole, splattered all over him, and the sound of the explosion seemed to fill up his body—the vibration, the force.

And then a wicked, screaming noise began—a sound like screeching animals. Yuki had heard about this. *Nebelwerfer*, the Germans called the weapon. "Smoke thrower." But Americans called it the "Screaming Mimi." Multiple mortars could be fired from a single rack in a constant bombardment, each shell shrieking with the same ferocity.

The men had been prepared for this—in lectures—but no words had communicated the terror Yuki was feeling now. He tried to make himself smaller, wished there were some way to cover his foxhole, to dig deeper, or, somehow, to escape and run.

The cordite smell from the explosions, the spreading smoke, the spray of falling dirt—all of it was getting inside Yuki, along with the noise and the shaking and swinging of the earth. It seemed more than he could stand much longer, but it kept going on and on.

For the better part of an hour the crashing never ceased, and every second Yuki thought the next explosion would be inside the foxhole with him and Shig. It seemed impossible that anyone could be alive out there, and just as impossible that he would survive.

And then everything stopped.

Yuki lay breathing for a time, hoping that was all for today. He was untouched except for the weakness in his muscles from holding himself so rigid. His brain and ears were still full of the chaos, and he couldn't see clearly, but he kept telling himself that he and Shig hadn't been hit. Maybe the barrage was over for now. That might mean a ground attack, but bullets seemed almost welcome after the big guns.

Yuki waited for a couple of minutes before he lifted himself a little, but Shig said, "Don't stand up yet."

"What?" Yuki thought his ears were ruined. He knew what Shig had said, but the words had seemed to come through a tunnel.

"You know what they taught us. The Germans give us time to go help our wounded and then they hit us again while we're out of our foxholes."

Yuki did remember that. But he also knew that some of his friends had to be dead. Or torn up and needing help.

Someone had begun to shout, "Medic! Medic! Help us."

Yuki stood up, tried to figure out where the sound had come from. He scanned the area, and then he saw that it was Mat's hole that had been turned into a crater, a shell having hit very close.

Yuki was halfway out of the hole when he heard the whistle of another shell, heard the shouts of "Incoming!" all over again. He dropped back into his hole for a moment. A second and third shell hit somewhere not too far away, but after that, the yelling started again. "Help us! Help us!"

It wasn't Mat's voice, but it was coming from that

vicinity, and Yuki knew he had to get there. As he scrambled out of his hole, he saw Hirinaka standing up, his helmet off and his head covered in blood. "I'll be okay!" he screamed at Yuki. "Help the sergeant."

Yuki dropped to his knees and looked into the foxhole. Mat was sitting up, staring toward Yuki but obviously not seeing him. His neck and shoulder were covered in blood.

"Mat, can you hear me?" Yuki yelled, but he got no answer.

Yuki slipped into the hole and stood over Mat with a foot on each side of him. He could see now that a hunk of metal was protruding from his shoulder, close to his neck. Blood was pumping out of him. Yuki glanced at Hirinaka, who was looking confused and battered himself. "Do you have any bandages?" Yuki shouted at him.

Hirinaka grabbed his pack, started to search through it. But shells were crashing around them again, shaking everything, making it hard to think.

Hirinaka found a bandage, tore the cover off it, and then pressed it to Mat's neck, fitting it around the piece of steel as best he could. But the blood was still coming. Yuki grabbed the bandage, pressed it. "Have you got another one?" he screamed.

"No."

"I've got to get him to an aid station. He's going to bleed to death."

Hirinaka's eyes came up, met Yuki's. He didn't say it

out loud, but clearly he didn't think Yuki could carry Mat that far.

"Help me get him out of here!" Yuki shouted, his words booming in the silence between explosions, but as Yuki tried to lift Mat—who was much heavier than Yuki—another shell struck not thirty yards away and Yuki was thrust back. He landed on Mat, looked into his eyes, saw nothing there, and then scrambled to his feet again, gripped his arms around Mat's torso, jerked him up with a powerful thrust. By then, Hirinaka was helping, and the two of them got Mat upright. Yuki let Hirinaka hold him, and he climbed out of the hole, reached down, put his hands under Mat's arms, and dragged him out onto the ground.

It didn't occur to Yuki that he couldn't lift the man. He just did it. Later, he thought maybe Hirinaka had helped—or some power greater than himself had done so. He got Mat over his shoulders in a fireman's carry, and then he ran—or stumbled—straight down through the field he had crossed the night before. Mat had said the CP was in that direction, off the crest of the hill, and that's where Yuki was heading. He knew all this was forcing blood from Mat's wound, but he could only think that he had to get his friend to a medic as fast as possible.

The noise around him was almost constant, the chaos, the raining clods of dirt, but Yuki's brain told him the fastest way was the straightest way and he charged ahead. Later, he remembered the hammering on his feet and legs, the pain in his shoulders, the sense of panic and terror. He even remembered Mat's blood soaking into his uniform. But as he ran, he thought of nothing except getting across the opening and off the hill. He never thought to slow down, even to yell for a medic.

And then a shell hit behind him and sent him tumbling forward. Mat rolled off Yuki's shoulders and flopped onto the ground. Yuki saw all the blood, the blank look on Mat's face, thought maybe he was dead, but he struggled frantically to get him upright again, and then he ducked under Mat's arm and, with a mighty thrust of his legs, stood up. Another shell struck behind him just as he was getting his balance, but he stumbled forward, and then ran again.

As Yuki came off the hill, he saw a soldier running toward him. He had a red cross on his helmet. "Medic," Yuki gasped, and he kept running until he'd made it around a little rise of earth that seemed enough cover from the shelling.

By then the medic had reached him. "Put him down!" the man shouted. "Let me have him."

Yuki couldn't put him down. He collapsed with Mat spread over him. The medic pulled him off Yuki, and then he went to work on the wound. Yuki didn't watch, didn't think. He only gulped for air. And then he rolled on his side and vomited.

It was a minute or so before he could think well enough, breathe well enough, to ask, "Is he still alive?"

"Yeah. For now. I've stopped the bleeding pretty much, and I'm getting plasma into him. But the concussion from the shell must have knocked him out. He's not coming around yet. I can't say for sure that he'll make it."

"Do something then!" Yuki screamed. He was suddenly furious. Mat couldn't die.

"I'm doing what I can, soldier. I can't—"

"I know. I know. But he needs to . . . he needs to live." Yuki had no idea what he meant by that. Only that Mat was a better man than most.

"I'll tell you one thing, Private. If you hadn't gotten him off that hill, he would've had no chance. But you never should have run across that field of fire. There's no way you should have survived that."

Yuki knew that and didn't know it. He felt the danger finally, but he hadn't thought about it at the time. Now he was feeling something wet on his leg, and he wondered whether he was bleeding. He touched his pant leg without looking at it, and the medic noticed. "It's water," he said, and he smiled.

"What?"

"Shrapnel must've cut a slit in your canteen. It emptied down your leg." He laughed. "That's a little too close."

"Yeah," Yuki said. But he didn't laugh. He was starting to realize that he had scrambled through falling shells and had run maybe three hundred yards with a guy bigger than himself over his shoulder. He was starting to understand that he couldn't have done that.

"I'm going to talk to the captain," the medic said. "I'm going to make sure you get a medal for this."

"No."

"What?"

"It's not like you think. I'm not brave."

"Don't tell me you're not brave. I saw what you did."

"Mat would've died," was all Yuki could think to say. "Don't tell the captain. He'll get the wrong idea." Yuki didn't want anyone to call him a hero. He knew better.

Up on the hill, the shells were still falling.

Yuki helped the medic carry Mat to the aid station at the CP. And then he waited for his chance to get back to Shig. But Captain Barker, the company commander, saw him start out and called to him, "Wait here, soldier. You can't make it back up there yet."

But what the captain didn't understand was that Shig was up there alone and had to be wondering what had happened to Mat and to Yuki. And all Yuki could think was that every foxhole must have been hit, and the entire platoon, the entire company, had surely been annihilated.

CHAPTER 10

The German artillery barrage continued off and on all morning. Yuki knew he was better off where he was, at the command post, but it felt wrong to him to be hunkered down in a safe place while his friends were taking a beating. Finally, in the afternoon, American artillery guns zeroed in on the German positions, and shells began to whoosh overhead, this time flying in the opposite direction. Before long, the German artillery attack began to let up, and German ground troops, which officers at the CP had expected all day, never appeared.

But the *Nisei* troops had paid a terrible price. Yuki had watched medics put themselves in danger at every cessation of the shelling, and he had seen way too many soldiers carried off the mountain. Yuki talked to a medic who said that since the beginning of the battle for Hill 140, the three rifle companies in Second Battalion—E,

F, and G—had taken more than 150 casualties, with 28 killed. Noncommissioned officers—the platoon sergeants and squad leaders—had been hit especially hard, and because few replacements were arriving, that meant inexperienced men would have to be promoted to take their leaders' places.

In the evening, artillery fire from both sides stopped and Yuki finally made his way back to his squad. He walked through the same open area he had run through that morning, but now there were craters everywhere and mounds of dirt cast in scattered bulges. As he got closer to the crest of the hill, he could see a big opening in the ground close to where he thought he and Shig had dug in. He slowed down, not wanting to see what he feared.

And then Shig was there, sitting on the edge of a foxhole a little left of the crater. As Yuki approached, Shig stared at him, his eyes too glazed to show much shock, but clearly confused.

"Are you all right?" Yuki asked.

Shig nodded, still staring, and then said, "I didn't think you made it off the hill."

"I shouldn't have," Yuki said. "Did we lose anyone up here?"

Shig looked away from Yuki. "Billy," he said, his voice little more than a whisper.

"Killed?"

"Yeah."

Yuki couldn't believe it. It didn't seem possible that Billy could suddenly stop existing. He wondered whether he should cry or scream or swear—do something. But the truth was, he felt more hollow than hurt. His brain couldn't seem to process death any more than it could comprehend what was going on around him. The world seemed to be blowing apart, and he was one of the people making it happen.

"Oki made it through. A shell ripped one end of their hole away. It tore up Billy really bad. Oki only got a few scratches, so the two of us worked on Billy, but he didn't have a chance. He only kept breathing for a few minutes."

"How's Oki handling it?"

"I don't know. I tried to talk to him a little while ago, but he's not saying a word."

"We've got to look out for him, Shig."

They didn't have to tell each other why. They knew what a friend Billy Yamada had been to Oki. But Yuki also thought of what Billy had lost. The war had taken away his chance to go to college, to be a star football player. Yuki had heard people use the phrase "lost his life" but he had never thought what it meant. Billy wouldn't have a chance to be the man he was going to be.

Don't think about it, Yuki told himself. *You can't think about it.*

"What about Mat?" Shig asked.

"He's alive. But he would have bled out if he hadn't

gotten to the CP." It was Yuki's way of saying that he was sorry he had left Shig alone.

"I don't know how you did it."

But Yuki had no idea how to talk about that. He hardly remembered his wild stumble down the hill. What he didn't want was any praise. At home, he had pictured himself as a hero, admired for his courage, but all he could think of now was the terror he had felt. "You're the guy who stuck it out up here," Yuki said. "That was the hardest thing."

Shig looked away. "It just wouldn't stop," he said.

Yuki understood the thousands of words that Shig wasn't saying. "I know. I kept thinking about you being alone up here. But the captain told me not to come back."

"I thought you were dead."

Shig ducked his head, put his hands over his face. Yuki turned away. He knew Shig was crying, but he pretended not to notice. Instead, Yuki looked down the slope. All he could think was that it was only a hill—just a bump on the planet—and hundreds of men had died or been mutilated fighting over it. He hadn't known about any of this before entering the army, hadn't understood what it would be like. What he wanted was to grab Shig and say, "Come on. Let's go home. Let's play some ball."

Lieutenant Freeman came along after a time. He asked Yuki to step aside with him. He stood close, which made him seem taller than ever. He told Yuki quietly, "You saved Sergeant Matsumoto's life. No question about that. But from now on, you have to measure the risk. By all odds, you ought to be dead."

"I know. But . . . he was bleeding bad."

"I understand. I respect you for doing it." He was smoking a cigarette. He took a last drag on it and then dropped the butt on the ground. "I guess you know about Don Fujii and Billy Yamada."

"Yeah."

"With Tahara gone, and now Yamada and Fujii, I'm going to collapse your squad's two fire teams into one five-man unit until we get replacements. I talked to Sergeant Oshira, and he wants you to lead the team. You'll get corporal stripes when we can get around to it."

"You don't need to make me a corporal. I don't know enough to get promoted."

The lieutenant studied him for a moment. "Look, Nakahara, you're younger than most of the men, and you're inexperienced—but so are the rest of us. I'm not saying that it was smart to run through all that artillery fire, but I'm glad you weren't willing to let your friend bleed to death. That's the attitude we need in the platoon."

Lieutenant Freeman sounded measured, even wise, but most of what the man knew about war he'd learned in the last few weeks. He'd gone to officers' school, but he had no more battle experience than Yuki had. All the same, Yuki liked that he didn't try to glorify Yuki's actions, didn't try to make him into something that he wasn't.

On the following morning, the 100th Battalion moved in and took over the position established by the Second Battalion. One of the soldiers from the 100th, a man who had clearly been through plenty of battles, told Yuki, "You guys soldias now. Hill one four puka mebby not Monte Cassino, but you do good."

"It only lasted a couple of days," Yuki told him. "From what I've heard, you guys were fighting at Monte Cassino a long time."

The private pulled his pack off his back and dropped it next to his feet. "We loss a lotta boys," he said. "Dat fo' sho. But you boys took mo' shells dan mos ennybody."

Yuki hadn't known that. He knew that he couldn't imagine anything worse, but he figured a guy who had been in the war for almost a year would claim he'd seen something bigger somewhere. It helped Yuki to think that he might not have to deal with anything quite so bad again.

The soldiers were allowed two days of rest. The Thirty-Fourth Division support troops brought a shower unit to the Cecina River, where the Four-Four-Two set up camp. Every soldier had a chance to get out of his old uniform and take a quick shower. They had been sweating in the summer heat and had slept in dirt for enough days that their uniforms were beyond filthy. In fact, the uniforms were burned, not washed. New uniforms were distributed, most of them once again too large. Then, on the shady side of a forested hill, the men rested, slept, cleaned their weapons, wrote letters home, and slept some more. Yuki was almost shocked by how quickly he and the other troops came back to life. On the second day, they actually joked a little, and the buddhaheads did some singing. But nothing felt loose now, and the laughter wasn't as careless as it had once been. For one thing, every man had lost friends. Yuki's platoon had lost about a third of its men, killed or wounded, and some platoons had lost more. But everyone had already learned that it was better not to talk about that.

Five letters caught up to Yuki at the rest camp: two from his mother, one each from May and Kay, and one from Keiko. He surprised himself by wanting to open Keiko's letter first, but he decided to save it until last. All of the letters were about the same. Life at Topaz was passable, even getting better, except that the heat was bad. Yuki could read between the lines that war was only an idea to all of them. It was just "the war"; there was no perception that wars were made of battles and bullets and one day following another. He wouldn't have known how to tell them what he was experiencing if he'd tried, and in the letters he sent back, he was vague about what he had done so far.

The men got their forty-eight hours of rest, and then they moved out. They marched all day through rolling hills. This was grassy country with few trees, and Yuki was soon sweating through his uniform again. The Germans had retreated, but he knew they would surely take another stand somewhere not too far off. For now, German artillerymen launched shells from distant emplacements, apparently for the sake of harassment. Most of the shells fell harmlessly off target, but the possibility of being hit kept the men wary.

Yuki dug in with Shig that evening, and then early in the morning, Sergeant Koba awakened them. At 0600, Fox Company led the attack on the Germans' new defensive position. First Platoon made the initial charge while Second Platoon—Yuki's unit—laid down heavy cover fire to keep the enemy as off balance as possible. Yuki could see muzzle fire from three machine guns, all guarded by a low rock wall that ran the length of an open field. Sergeant Oshira instructed his squad to zero in on the gun to the right, and the five men blasted the area with their M1 rifles. American mortar teams were also firing at will, the thumps continuous, and automatic weapons from both sides filled the air with streaking tracer bullets.

First Platoon dropped down after their charge and laid down their own barrage of fire. As soon as that happened,

Second Platoon, on Lieutenant Freeman's command, jumped to their feet and attacked. They stayed spread out, fired from the hip as they charged, and ran past First Platoon's position. But the German machine-gun fire was heavier now, more accurate. A man to Yuki's left took a hit and went down. And then a mortar shell struck close and Yuki saw men fall, scream. With every step Yuki expected that a bullet would take him down, but he kept going, and when Sergeant Koba dropped to the ground and aimed his rifle, so did the rest of the platoon.

Now First Platoon was up and moving again. Second Platoon could fire with better effect on the machine guns now, and the center gun suddenly went silent. But German mortars were striking constantly.

The two platoons leapfrogged again. A lot of men had gone down, and two machine guns were still pumping out bullets, the sound of them like electricity sizzling in the air. When the machine gun straight ahead of Yuki suddenly stopped, he hoped the German gunners had been knocked out, but it was just as likely that they had stopped only to reload. Still, he knew the break in the fire was an opportunity to make a move.

Yuki jumped up and bolted to his right. He covered about thirty yards before the machine gun started to fire again, the bullets zinging past him. He dove down behind some brush, and the men of his platoon continued to direct heavy fire at the emplacement. The Germans, in response, swung their aim back toward the main body of the platoon.

Yuki knew that men were getting hit. He couldn't let this go on much longer. He pulled a grenade from his belt, jumped up, and ran back to the left, directly toward the emplacement. He made it to within thirty yards or so, when he saw tracer bullets flying past him again. He dove to the ground, pulled the pin on the grenade, and then lofted it toward the machine gun. His breath held as he waited, and then the explosion sent debris flying. Yuki jumped up immediately and charged again. He leaped over the little rock fence and into the emplacement, his weapon ready. Four men were down, two of them alive, staring at him.

For a moment everything held. The men didn't move, only watched to see what Yuki might do.

"*Hände hoch!*" Yuki yelled, almost the only words he had learned in German. "Hands high."

One of the men held up one hand, and Yuki saw that his other arm was lying limp at his side. "Don't shoot," he said in English.

The other soldier made an effort and raised both hands slightly above his shoulders, but he looked stunned, hardly aware of what was going on. Yuki watched both men who were alive and at the same time glanced at the other two. He knew he couldn't assume for certain that they were dead.

By then American soldiers were streaming toward the emplacement, jumping the little wall, aiming their weapons at the two Germans holding up their hands. Yuki realized that the other machine gun had stopped and the mortar fire had also stopped.

"They're retreating!" someone yelled. "Keep 'em running."

A lot of men moved on past the wall and the ridge behind it. Yuki heard firing again, but he could tell that the bullets were aimed at the fleeing Germans.

Sergeant Koba soon stepped over the wall. "Good job, Nakahara," he said.

Yuki liked the praise, but he realized he was quivering now and his pulse was racing.

"You deal with these men," Sergeant Koba said. "Take them back to the CP for interrogation." He walked over and used his foot to roll one of the apparently dead men on his side, and then stared down at the other one, who was lying on his back. "These two are finished." He took a better look at Yuki. "You okay?" he asked.

"Yeah. I think so. I'm not hit or anything like that."

"Maybe not. But you don't look good."

Yuki tried to laugh. "I always thought I was pretty good looking," he said.

Sergeant Koba didn't smile. He continued to watch Yuki. "You did what you had to do," he said. "I'm proud of you."

Koba was older than any of the men in the platoon, and Yuki always knew that he cared about the "kids" he was leading. It meant a lot to know that the sergeant was pleased with him. Emotion was still pounding through his body—fear and exhilaration at the same time—but it was Koba's gentle praise that affected Yuki most. He realized that he was on the verge of breaking down, and he couldn't let that happen. So he straightened, and tried to sound stern when he told the two Germans, "Stand up. *Now.*"

The soldier who had spoken English used his good arm to help himself stand, and then he helped the other man get up. "Can he walk?" Yuki asked.

"I help him. Don't shoot."

"I won't shoot you unless you try something. Help him over that wall." He pointed back across the field of battle. "We're going that way."

The soldier nodded, but he took a long look, as though realizing that Yuki wasn't what he had expected. The German had handsome eyes, dark blue, but they were tired, lifeless. "Thank you," he said. "Please not shoot us."

"Just step over that wall," he said. "Help your friend."

The soldier nodded again, but he still didn't move. "You make us in prison?"

"Yes."

"*Gut.* No more war for us. You give us food?"

"Yes."

"Das ist auch gut." And still he continued to stare at Yuki. "You Chinese?"

"No. Japanese."

"Why you go war for America?"

"Because I'm an American," he said.

"But you—"

"Step over that wall. Right now. Don't ask me any more questions."

The man nodded, accepted. He helped his friend over the wall, and then he held him up as they walked, while Yuki walked behind them. "I'm an American," he muttered again. He told himself he didn't have to prove that from now on—to himself or to anyone else. He had taken out a machine-gun nest. That was the kind of stuff heroes did. But then, he wondered, why were his hands still shaking? Why did he feel on the edge of falling apart?

Still, he delivered the Germans to the intelligence officer at the CP, and then he turned back to find his platoon. There were still a number of bodies lying on the ground. Some had been marked and would be carried away later. The ones whose faces he could see were almost all people he knew, some of them friends. A man named Aiso, who had joined the army with him at Topaz, was lying on his back, a bullet hole in his chest and blood staining the front of his uniform. Yuki and Shig had worked with Aiso back in the sugar beet fields of Utah. Yuki knew the guy's family, knew he had a girlfriend who had promised to wait for him.

In the middle of the meadow, he saw a medic working on a man who was bigger than most of the *Nisei*. Yuki walked closer, hoping he was wrong but gradually recognizing that it was Oki. He hurried over, ran the last few steps.

The medic was working on Oki's legs. It looked like he'd been shot in both thighs. One leg was bandaged. The medic had cut the pant leg away on the other and was wrapping the wound.

"Oki, are you okay?" Yuki asked.

"Not too bad."

"I gave him a shot of morphine," the medic told Yuki.

"How bad is he hurt?"

"I don't know for sure. I think the femur is broken in this leg. I don't think he'll be back on the line."

"That's good, Oki," Yuki said. "You're going to get out of here. You got yourself a million-dollar wound."

"Guess so."

But Yuki could see what the war, after only a month, had done to Oki. He saw none of the old lightness. "I'll look you up when I get home," Yuki said. "I'll come to Hawaii. We'll have a good time."

"Yeh. Sho thing. You good man, Yuki."

"But you betta," Yuki said. He tried to laugh, but he couldn't manage it.

Oki was reaching out by then. Yuki grasped his hand, held it for a moment. He thought of the two Germans who just wanted to eat, to survive, to get home. Oki was not so different from them. It struck Yuki as almost comic that humans drew lines on the globe, and on both sides of those lines raised up armies. Then they fought and died to take possession of . . . what? Hills. Yuki knew he had to fight, and had to win, but that didn't make war anything to be proud of.

CHAPTER II

For an entire week the Germans continued to retreat. Yuki's battalion chased them across hills and vineyards and through villages. Lieutenant Freeman informed his men that the battalion officers believed the Germans were falling back to the Arno River, near Florence. That may have been true, but along the way, they were attempting to inflict as much damage on the Allied troops as they could. There were plenty of tough fights for the *Nisei* soldiers as the Germans set up ambushes or left behind snipers to pick off Americans one at a time.

As the troops continued to move ahead, pockets of enemy soldiers had to be engaged and forced to retreat northward or captured. After a skirmish in a little town one day, members of Fox Company were moving through the streets, checking houses in search of German soldiers who might be hiding in attics or wine cellars. After Yuki and Shig inspected one house, an older couple, clearly relieved that their town had been liberated, thanked Yuki and Shig profusely and offered them each a glass of wine. They drank the wine, accepted the embraces of the man and woman, and started down the street. But just then they heard the whoosh of an incoming shell.

Yuki and Shig automatically dove toward the street, but the shell struck the cobblestones in front of them before they were down. Yuki felt the blast hit his eyes. He curled up in the street and held his hands over his face, but after a few seconds, when he took his hands away and tried to see, everything was a blur. Still, he knew he had to get out of the street. He raised himself up on his knees, felt for Shig and got hold of his jacket. "Are you okay?" Yuki asked.

"I don't know."

"We gotta move. Can you see?"

"No."

They managed to stand up, clung to each other, and stumbled off the street to a house, and then Yuki felt his way into a little alley that he remembered was on the south side. By then, his vision was clearing a little. Tears were flowing, washing the grit from his eyes. He and Shig sat down, their backs to the wall, and Shig said, "I can see a little now. But I'm bleeding. Pretty bad."

Yuki was feeling stinging pain, and he looked at his hands to see the dirt and blood that had come off his face.

"The splintered stones from the street got us," he said. "I don't think we took any shrapnel."

Shig was looking at Yuki by then. "You're all cut up," he said.

"You too." But the good news was, he could now see quite well. "We need to doctor each other up as much as we can."

But as usual, a medic showed up rather quickly. He had obviously heard the shell hit and had come looking to see whether there were casualties. Shig saw him hurry past the alley and yelled out to him, "Hey, in here!"

The man was back in seconds. He dropped to his knees between Yuki and Shig. "Where are you hit?" he asked.

"We took some debris on our faces, that's all," Yuki said. "We're not hurt bad."

The medic had water with him. He used it to wash away the dirt, and then he bandaged the cuts. He worked quickly and then said, "Okay. I want you two to fall back. There's an aid station just south of town. They'll patch you up a little better, and then you need a few days to rest and heal. All right?"

"Sure," Yuki said.

"Are you okay to find your way back on your own? I heard rifle fire up the street. I've got to see who else might be hit."

"We're fine. Go ahead."

The medic assembled his materials and stood up.

"Thanks for getting here so fast," Yuki said. "What's your name?"

"Jones." He smiled. "I'm only half Japanese."

"Where are you from?"

"Tacoma, Washington."

"Are you a doctor or—"

"No. But I want to be. Do you think I can get into medical school after serving over here?"

"Why not?" Yuki said. "Being named Jones should help."

They all laughed, and Jones ran back to the street.

Yuki and Shig were still sitting on the ground, their backs against the rock wall of the house. Neither moved for a time. Finally Shig said, "Are you going back to the aid station?"

"I don't know. I guess it depends on what you're going to do." But Yuki did know. He wasn't going back just because he had a few cuts on his face—not unless Shig felt he needed to get fixed up. "Are you going back?"

"No. Too many guys are down already. We need everyone up front."

That was the answer. He wasn't at all surprised that Shig felt the same way. "But we need a couple of minutes," Yuki said.

"Yeah."

And so they sat a little longer, and Yuki told himself that it wasn't wrong to have a breather. There were men taking fire not far away, and he and Shig needed to get there, but his face was hurting, his ears were ringing, and he still couldn't see as well as he wanted to. He needed this peace, this chance to feel safe behind a rock house for just a few minutes.

Yuki looked down the alley. It ended with a rock wall; one could get trapped here. He tested to see how his eyes were adjusting, took a look out to where the alley opened onto the street. What he saw was a stucco house with a red tile roof, dark moss growing over everything. On the main level of the house was a little shop with barrels lined up in front, and on top of the tallest barrel was a tortoise-shell cat, napping in the sun. Either the cat had not been run off by the artillery shell, or it had already returned and wasn't worried about soldiers in the streets.

Yuki had seen pictures of Europe all his life—on calendars and travel posters. He had never expected to see a village as picturesque as this. But he hadn't really looked at the town, didn't even know the name of it. He had only watched doors, listened for movement, feared the possibility of a tank hidden on some side street. He longed to have time to really *see* what he had been seeing, but he could only look from this alley. Once he was back on the street, he would have to think as a soldier again.

Shig was saying, "We better get going."

"Yeah." But they didn't move.

Shig was sitting back, apparently thinking, not gazing

about as Yuki had been doing. He surprised Yuki by saying, "There's something I've been wondering about lately."

"What's that?"

"Are you still thinking you want to marry my sister?"

Yuki looked over at Shig. He had sounded serious, but he was smiling a little. "What about you? Are you still worried that I will?"

"Well, I'll tell you the truth. I hope you two do get married. We'd be brothers-in-law, so we'd stay in touch all our lives."

"Yeah. That'd be good. Of course, we might not . . ."

"What?"

"You know what."

"You don't think we'll make it home, do you?"

"Do you?"

"I don't know. Everyone's getting hit. It seems like the only way out of here is the way Oki did it."

"Even getting shot doesn't always work. They patch up a lot of guys and send them back to the line. The only hope for getting home, as far as I can see, is if we get shot up pretty bad. Keiko won't want me if I come home all messed up."

Shig seemed to consider that. Finally he said, "She likes you a lot. She told me that in the last letter I got from her. I think she wanted me to tell you." Suddenly Shig smiled again. "But I gotta admit, she might not feel that way if she could get a look at you right now."

Yuki looked at Shig, saw the tape and bandages criss-crossing his face. "I think you're right—if I look like you."

"What's she telling you, Yuki? Does she say she wants to wait for you?"

"Nah. She's never said anything like that. She talks about the dances at camp, and a soda fountain they've built there now. She's still a kid, Shig. She's not thinking about getting married."

"I'm not so sure about that. She's almost eighteen now. She said that we're heroes back at the camp. And you know how girls are. They like that kind of stuff." He gave Yuki a little slug on the shoulder. "Especially if the guy is also a good dancer."

"I'll tell you what. You marry May, and then we'll be double brothers-in-law. How would that be?"

But Shig didn't smile about this. "I'd like that, but May would never be interested in me."

"Why not?"

"Girls don't pay attention to me. That's not going to change whether I'm a hero or not."

"Come on, Shig. You're the best guy I've ever known. Girls are going to know that. It's not just . . . you know . . ."

"What? Not just that I'm so lanky?"

"Hey, we're all short. That doesn't matter." Yuki wanted to tell Shig how mild and good he was, but he couldn't say something like that. He only said, "You're the best friend anyone could have. You'll find someone who sees that."

Shig shrugged, as though he weren't really convinced. "First, we gotta figure out a way to keep ourselves alive," he said.

Yuki looked across the alley at the sidewall of another rock house. There was something wonderful about this safe place between two walls where no shells were likely to drop. He wished he could just stay right here until the war was over. He thought of Keiko, wondered whether he would ever see her again, and if he did, when that might be.

But when he thought of her, he felt the discomfort he had been trying to deal with lately. It was something he had not talked to Shig about, and he hadn't thought he would, but he found himself admitting, "Keiko is so innocent. I don't think I'm worthy of her anymore."

"Why? What do you mean?"

"I don't know. I just don't feel good about what we do every day."

"We're just doing what has to be done."

"I know. I get that. We have to win this war, no matter what it takes. But I know who I was . . . and I think I know what I'll be before this is all over. You ought to knock me over the head if I ever come near your sister. I'm not good enough for her."

"That's not true. We can't let it be true." Neither spoke for a time, but then Shig added, "But I know what you mean. You can't wade through this much muck and still feel like you can wash it all off afterward."

That was it. What he and Shig were doing—and the Germans, too—was brutal, disgusting. Killing was killing, no matter how hard people tried to redefine it. Yuki knew he would have to spend his life trying to remove all this ugliness from his head and hands.

The two got up and walked out of the alley and then back up the street that a few minutes before had blown up in their faces. And from there, they walked back to the fight.

Yuki and Shig, with their unit, fought their way across the plains of Pisa and reached the Arno River. They stayed close to one another during every march, every attack, and they spent each night together in a foxhole.

At the Arno, the 442nd entered into a standoff with the enemy. American soldiers did not expect the Germans to counterattack back across the river, and they didn't know when their own officers would order them to make that crossing themselves. But the forward push didn't happen, and the 442nd received word that they were being pulled off the line for a few days of rest. R&R was a welcome change, of course, but for the first couple of days, it was hard on the nerves. Yuki would fall asleep quickly, only to awaken at the slightest sound, and then he would not go back to sleep easily. He noticed that his fellow soldiers still laughed, and drank any alcohol they could get their hands on, but they were not talkative now, at least not about the war.

They did write letters home, and now their mail caught up to them again. Yuki got a letter from Keiko, which was full of her teenage talk about things happening at the camp, and lots of praise for the bravery of the Japanese American troops. He also heard from his mother, who expressed her love for him, and her pride in his valor. He hardly knew how to think about that, but the words brought tears to his eyes; he hoped so much that he would see her again.

Replacement soldiers were arriving now, and Yuki's platoon was being rebuilt. But the new guys seemed loud and full of themselves. Yuki found himself avoiding them. He was well aware that a few months back he had been much like them, but battle experiences changed everything. The guys coming in hadn't seen their friends killed yet, and they hadn't killed. The war games they had been playing back in the States would be turning real soon, and they would lose their arrogance—if they lived that long.

A young guy named Denny Saito was assigned to a tent with Yuki and Shig. He came in full of questions about what to expect and what the platoon had accomplished so far. Yuki didn't want to act like a big shot, and he knew Shig felt the same way. They explained only briefly where they had fought so far, and they made a point of letting him understand that many of their friends had been killed or wounded.

"Allied troops have broken out from the beaches in Normandy now," Private Saito told them. "They're moving fast. They'll drive the Germans out of France this fall. I don't think the war will last until Christmas."

Yuki was sitting on a cot in the six-man tent. He thought of getting up and walking out. He didn't want to scare the kid, but he also knew that Saito couldn't go into battle thinking the war was over. "The Germans are still fighting hard," he said. "Don't underestimate them. They're well trained and they have effective weapons. They're fighting to save their homeland now, and they won't just lay down their rifles and let us walk on in."

"You sound like you're scared of 'em. Us guys coming in are—"

"Watch yourself, Private."

The young man was sitting on another cot, his knees almost touching Yuki's. He had the look of a bulldog, his cheeks a bit droopy and his bottom teeth biting over the top ones. But his eyes were wide open, and he was clearly shocked at Yuki's sudden change of tone. Yuki had heard the anger in his own voice, and he let himself calm for a few seconds before he said, "Replacements who think they know everything are the ones most likely to get themselves killed. So watch the rest of us and keep your head down. Don't—"

"How am I supposed to shoot Krauts with my head down?"

Yuki took a long breath. He didn't want to be too hard on the guy. "Look," he said, "we haven't been here all that long either, but we've been through a lot of battles, and we've learned some things. There's a difference between being brave and being a fool. Just watch the guys who know what they're doing and don't try to be a hotshot."

"I didn't come over here to duck my head, Corporal Nakahara."

Yuki lowered his eyes, couldn't think what to say.

But Shig said, "Let me tell you something, Private. A while back a friend of ours named Billy Yamada got hit by an artillery shell. He only lived a few minutes, but the whole time he was conscious he was crying and calling for his mother. He was a tough guy. Nothing scared him. He attacked a machine-gun nest all by himself in one of our first battles. But at the end, he wanted his mama, like a little kid does when he's sick."

Yuki had never heard this before. Shig hadn't told him. Saito looked solemn.

"You don't know what it's like yet," Shig said. "You just don't know how you'll react until you're in the thick of things. It's best not to say too much until you do know."

A glow of light was shining through the canvas of the tent. The air was close, filled with the smell of boots that had been wet over and over, and uniforms that had been full of sweat and dirt too many times. Saito was silent, clearly taking in the things Shig had said.

Yuki suddenly felt sorry for him. "Well, anyway," he said, "we'll help you along, but you have to be willing to learn from the rest of us."

"I'm not saying I won't be scared. I'm just—"

But right then someone lifted a flap of the tent and stuck his head in. Just as Yuki realized who it was, Shig said, "Mat! What are you doing back here?"

"I missed you guys," Sergeant Matsumoto said, and he laughed. Then he bent and stepped into the tent. But his motion seemed out of balance, his shoulder stiff.

"I thought they were sending you home," Yuki said.

"They wanted me to ship out, but I wouldn't do it. I went AWOL from the hospital. But I figure if they find me up here, the worst they can do is shoot me. It's the same thing the Germans keep trying to do. What's the difference?" He hesitated and took a longer look at Shig and Yuki. "Hey, what happened to you guys?"

"We got in a fight and scratched each other's faces," Yuki said. He laughed. "Like a couple of cats."

But Shig was asking, "Why come back? You didn't have to."

"I didn't want to go home while the rest of the platoon was still fighting. I just felt guilty about doing that."

Yuki looked over at Saito. He was glad to see the look of admiration on the boy's face.

Mat looked at Private Saito too. "Yuki here carried me off a hill. He ran through the middle of an artillery barrage that should have killed both of us—and I'm about twice his size. I'd be dead now if he hadn't gotten me to an aid station." Then he looked at Yuki. "I figure I owe you one. I came back to do the same for you if the need ever comes up." He smiled, nodded. "But I hope it doesn't."

Yuki looked back at Saito one more time. "Like I said, learn from the guys who've been around for a little while. We take care of each other."

"You told me not to take chances."

"Well, sometimes we do—for each other."

Saito nodded, and he didn't say another word.

CHAPTER 12

October 1944

Yuki was in France. After the troops had rested a few days in August, they had been trucked back to the Arno River. Soon after, however, the Four-Four-Two, along with the 100th Battalion, was transported to the port of Piombino, where they were conveyed by ship to Naples. There, they boarded another ship and sailed to Marseilles, in the south of France.

Yuki never understood the thinking of the generals who moved troops around. But he did know from reading *Stars and Stripes*, the army newspaper, that shortly after D-Day, when the Allies had landed in Normandy on the west coast of France, a second front had been opened in southern France. Those who had landed in the west had now taken Paris and were pushing on across France. The southern attack had driven Germans northward, but now, as forces converged on Germany, the fight had become intense, and Yuki assumed that the 442nd had been brought in to help smash the German defense. What most of Yuki's friends believed was that military leaders now considered their unit one of the best, able to break through when others couldn't. And it was not just the 100th Battalion that was considered elite, but the entire Four-Four-Two.

Yuki knew that the south coast of France was a place to vacation, but he also guessed, correctly, that he would not be there long. What he hadn't expected was almost constant rain. Even worse, as trucks carried the men northward, the rain and cold continued. The long hours in the back of a jolting, jostling truck were tedious, but by October 11, the men had set up camp near the Vosges Forest in eastern France, not far from the Rhine River, which formed the border with Germany.

The terrain in this part of France was different from the land the 442nd had occupied in Italy. The forests were filled with spreading French oaks and long-needled pines some seventy feet high; the dense growth created a full canopy overhead. The men camped one night under these dark trees. They dug foxholes and then covered them with shelter halves—small tents, two halves of which snapped together at the top. But there was no staying dry. The rain dribbled through the trees' canopy, and water ran everywhere, working its way into the foxholes and turning the ground, in and out of the holes, into heavy mud. The men were still wearing summer uniforms, the army not having supplied them yet with winter coats and boots, so they suffered just getting through the night.

The 442nd had been away from battle for over a month, but what Lieutenant Freeman now announced was that Second Battalion would make a thrust toward Bruyères in the morning. He told the men that Bruyères was a crossroads town, with several roads and a railroad line all converging there, and it was held by the Germans. It was the key town that needed to be cleared before pushing on to the Rhine. "We can't just charge into Bruyères," the lieutenant told the men. "We have to take the high ground on the hills around the place. Our battalion, along with Third Battalion, will have to push the enemy off Hill B on the north side of town."

Fox Company soldiers had managed to scrounge more firepower. Some of them had Browning automatic rifles and others had Thompson submachine guns. By now, the troops also knew how to work together, how to cover for one another, how to lay down a fierce field of fire that could overwhelm the enemy.

After Lieutenant Freeman explained the strategy of the attack, Sergeant Koba had some things to add. "The battalion officers are telling us this is going to be a cakewalk. But I think the Germans are lying low. When we attack, if we don't meet much resistance, don't get overconfident. Bruyères is too important for the Germans to give up easy. I think these hills are full of Krauts."

But at 0800 that morning, everything began the way the battalion leaders had predicted. The march started in the dark forest, and all was quiet. The rain had stopped, but the trees continued to drip, keeping the men's uniforms soaked. The men advanced toward Hill B and then began a gradual ascent. Yuki hoped there would be no resistance after all. But just when he had begun to relax, everything changed—suddenly and violently.

A line of German soldiers sprang up out of the ground. They cast off limbs and greenery that they had used to cover their slit trench, and they opened fire. Machine pistols started first, and in only a few seconds, machine gunners began to fill the forest with their racket, the bullets striking trees, ripping through the underbrush.

The *Nisei* troops dropped down, found cover behind trees. But Sergeant Koba was shouting, "Don't fall back! Go after them!"

Yuki didn't charge directly into the fire, but he followed Sergeant Oshira's example: He broke to the cover of a nearby tree, fired his rifle in a quick burst, hid until he'd stopped drawing fire, and then made another quick run forward. Yuki's fire team followed and used the same method of advance. By then the enemy fire was not just from the line of soldiers in the slit trench; German mortars and heavy artillery had begun to pound the forest.

Yuki hunkered down as shells hit high in the trees and sent shrapnel and broken tree limbs, like spears, crashing around him.

Sergeant Koba was shouting again. "Don't stop! Keep going!" And Yuki understood. To stop was to wait for the artillery to fill the forest with flying steel. He rushed ahead, took aim, and fired at a machine gun. Then he dropped again, waited a few seconds, and made another quick dash. He spotted Shig, Higa, and Tanna—all working their way closer to the Germans like he was. And young Private Saito was staying with Shig, making the same moves.

Yuki was about to break forward again when he heard something new. A German land mine—a "Bouncing Betty"—clanked as it released. Yuki glanced over just as the mine jumped a few feet into the air and detonated. The explosion tore into a man's groin and torso. The soldier—one of the replacements—folded in on himself, slumped to the ground, and then let out a deep groan.

Yuki knew that medics would move in as soon as they could to help the guy. For now, the platoon had to keep driving ahead. But every step was dangerous. Yuki had no idea how many land mines might be out there in the woods. Somewhere in the midst of all the noise and smoke, he heard another clank, another mine explode. At the same time, shells were still dropping into the trees. It was like walking through hell, with fire from the earth and sky, the noise deafening, the smoke and flying debris blurring everything.

But the *Nisei* soldiers were also taking a toll on the line of defense in front of them. From the cover of the trees, the Americans were firing their rifles and automatic weapons, and many of the Germans had gone down. The intense return fire was gradually diminishing, and then, suddenly, the defensive line broke. The Germans began leaping from their trench and running into the forest, some of them dropping as the Americans continued to fire at them.

The AJA soldiers ran to the trench and Sergeant Koba yelled for his platoon to hold up. Yuki jumped into the trench, then looked around to watch for his men. All of the soldiers in his fire team were all right, and Yuki spotted Mat. But he thought that five or six from the platoon had gone down, maybe more. He could see a number of soldiers on the ground, under the trees; medics were moving up to help them.

Yuki worked his way through the trench, past some other men and over to Shig. "Are you okay?" he asked.

Shig nodded. "I'm thinking they might send us forward again, once we rest a little."

Yuki knew that, but the two sat down in the trench, leaned back, let themselves catch their breath.

After a few minutes Shig said, "We lost Kikuchi, from Mat's squad. Shrapnel ripped up his face and neck—really bad."

Yuki didn't say anything. Shig knew the man better than Yuki did.

"He was one of the smartest guys I've ever—"

"Is he dead?"

"Yeah. I'm sure he is."

"Then there's no use talking about him."

"I just—"

"I know. But don't tell me anything else. I don't want to know." Yuki realized that he sounded angry, and he didn't want to talk that way to Shig. He softened his voice and said, "I just don't want to have him on my mind. You understand what I'm saying, don't you?"

"Sure."

But Yuki knew the truth. He would be thinking about these guys the rest of his life, even the ones he hadn't known too well.

After a time, Sergeant Koba spread the word that the platoon would stop where it was for the rest of the day. Yuki thought that was a bad decision. He was relieved not to push ahead, but it seemed to him they should keep the Germans on the run.

The men rested, ate, waited. The rain had started again, and the trench soon began collecting water. Yuki and Shig, like most of the men, sat on their helmets to stay out of the mud, and after a time they all began gathering the brush the Germans had used to cover the trench. They even cut down saplings to stiffen the "roof" they were creating. Most of the men had shelter halves with them, and they wrapped up in those and tried, as dark settled in, to stay dry and warm, but the cold was miserable, and Yuki's feet were freezing. He knew his socks were wet. The medics always told the men they had to change stockings every day and put the wet ones inside their uniforms, under their arms, where the wool could dry. But it wasn't easy to change socks in a muddy hole or to dry them inside a wet uniform. Yuki sensed that trench foot—the decaying of tissue caused by dampness and cold—would now be as much an enemy as German bullets. He knew he needed to change his stockings soon, but he didn't want to unwrap himself in the cold. He vowed to do it in the morning.

As it turned out, the battle for Hill B continued for three days, and every inch of ground had to be taken the same way: the men attacking through the forest in short bursts against withering fire. More men in the platoon and company were going down each day, but Yuki was relieved that his own fire team was still untouched. Then on October 18, the battalion pushed the German troops out of their position at the top of the hill, and on the same day, other American forces took the town of Bruyères.

Yuki was hurting by the time the troops settled in on the high ground. He had finally changed his socks, but the rain had continued, off and on, all through the battles, and he never really got his spare stockings dry. His feet had begun to sting and ache, so he knew that he could be in trouble before long. Still, there was no chance to do much about it. After two nights of rest in the cold and wet, the battalion was ordered to move deeper into the Vosges Forest and take another hill, this one called Hill D.

What the *Nisei* faced this time was the same challenge as before: an entrenched enemy occupying higher ground, and a dense forest to penetrate. As they began to advance through the trees, they were pinned down by fire from the top of the hill. But they didn't turn back. They slowly worked their way through the forest toward the crest of the hill until they reached the edge of a clearing. Faced with machine-gun emplacements on the high side of the clearing, they stopped. Minutes passed, and Yuki saw the difficulty. German tanks and artillery could zero in and shell them. Mortars were likely to start hitting them at any moment. He knew the platoon had to either drop back quickly or make a hard drive forward. Someone had to decide.

It was Sergeant Koba who suddenly charged into the clearing carrying a Thompson submachine gun. He concentrated his fire on one of the emplacements at the top of the clearing. The German gun fell silent, and Yuki was about to charge forward with his fire team, but in the same instant, Koba was struck by German fire and he tumbled backward down the hill. Yuki saw him fall and was about to run to him, but men who were closer were already going after him. Two of those men were hit immediately, and the others fell back.

No one moved. The men of Second Platoon had seen their platoon sergeant go down, and they had seen some of their brothers riddled with bullets while they were trying to help him. Yuki and Shig were lying flat behind a big pine tree. "We can't just stay here," Shig said.

Yuki knew that, but someone had moved into the clearing with a white flag, and four men with red crosses on their helmets—medics—carried litters and ran toward the sergeant and the other wounded men. One pair worked on Sergeant Koba for only a few seconds and then shifted him onto a litter, while the other medics looked after the other two men who had gone down.

As the medics lifted Sergeant Koba and began to carry him away, a sniper bullet buzzed through the air. Yuki saw Sergeant Koba hunch—shot through the body while lying on the litter. Now more rifles were firing, and one of the medics dropped to the ground.

Yuki felt a crazy rage fill his head. The Germans couldn't do that. They couldn't shoot medics, couldn't shoot wounded men on litters. He knew he had to kill someone.

He jumped up, and just as he did, he saw Sergeant Oshira charge into the clearing. He had a Browning automatic rifle slung under his arm, and he was firing it on automatic, spreading bullets at the entrenched forces up above. And that was all the men of the platoon needed to see. As though by signal, they charged out of their cover and broke into the clearing, all of them shooting, the noise constant and thundering.

Yuki ran forward, firing his rifle, only one thing in mind. He would make it to the top of the hill and he would kill all the Germans he could. "Banzai!" someone shouted, and everyone picked up the old Japanese cry. Yuki bellowed the word and kept running. He felt like a samurai warrior. Nothing was going to stop him.

The charge up the hill was more chaos than precision. The air seemed full of bullets, slapping into the ground around Yuki, or flying past him. But he didn't care. The roar from both sides was incessant, and even though men were falling, no one took cover. Every man who still had legs under him kept going, and the enemy fire slowed, then stopped. Yuki could see German soldiers jumping from foxholes and machine-gun nests, and running farther up the hill into the dense trees.

It was all over in a few minutes, and suddenly everything was quiet. But Yuki wanted more. He kept running, looked for someone to shoot. He finally saw a German soldier cowering near a tree, an easy target.

Yuki aimed carefully and squeezed the trigger . . . or at least he tried. But he couldn't do it. He dropped the rifle down, thought for a moment, then told himself he *had* to do it—for Sergeant Koba. He aimed again, actually strained to tighten his finger around that trigger . . . and failed again.

The German's helmet was gone, and blood was running from his head down his neck. His face was distorted, his eyes full of confusion and despair. Yuki's anger was seeping away. He still wanted to shoot someone, but he knew he couldn't kill this man.

The German finally slumped to the ground, maybe dead. Yuki didn't know what to feel about that. He wanted to run after the retreating Germans, somehow find the one who had shot Sergeant Koba, and then have his revenge. But he was still watching the wounded soldier. He started to walk toward him. He knew he couldn't just leave him there to die. When he got to the man, he turned him over and saw that a bullet had pierced his head just above his ear and had broken away a hunk of his skull.

Shig walked up close. "He's dead," he said. "I hope he was the one who shot Sergeant Koba."

"I don't think it was this guy," Yuki told him, but he didn't know why he felt that way.

The two of them kept staring at the man, the gruesome damage to his head. A few months back, such a sight would have made Yuki sick. But he had seen plenty since then, and the wound itself meant nothing to him. What he was remembering was the desperate look he had seen on the man's face. It was what had stopped him from shooting.

"I don't understand the Krauts," Shig said. "Who could shoot a man on a litter?"

But Yuki knew something that Shig didn't. Yuki had come within a breath of pulling his own trigger. *He* could have killed a man who was down and wounded, just hoping to survive. "Most of 'em wouldn't do that," he said. "But war does things to people. They get crazy."

"Shoot medics? I could never do that."

"I know. You couldn't."

"You're bleeding, Yuki."

"I know."

Somewhere on the hill he had felt the sharp sting of a bullet as it sliced his arm above his elbow.

"Walk back to where I left my pack. Let me look at it."

So the two walked to the place where the Germans had been dug in. *Nisei* soldiers were all around now. Some were still letting out their anger, swearing, cursing the Germans. Others were sitting, breathing—utterly exhausted. And some were on their way back down the hill to help the wounded.

Shig helped Yuki take his jacket off, and then they looked at the wound. It was bleeding, but it wasn't deep— a slice maybe two inches long. In the past Yuki would have thought how close he had come, how easily he could have been killed, but he wasn't thinking about that now. He was thinking of the new reality for the platoon. Sergeant Koba was gone.

"You need to go down and get this bandaged," Shig was saying.

"Just do it yourself. It's not serious."

"You could get an infection if it's not cleaned up right."

"Just slap something on there. It's okay."

"You'll get a Purple Heart."

"No. I won't take a medal for a cut on my arm. The sergeant is the one who deserves all the medals."

CHAPTER 13

Shig finished bandaging the cut on Yuki's arm, and then the two tried to settle down and relax for a few minutes. After the charge up the hill—and after the rage—Yuki was feeling spent. He lay back on the wet grass and shut his eyes. His feet were burning, and the cuts on his face were still sore. His arm wasn't hurting much yet, but he was sure it would before long. What he also knew was that he would sleep in mud again that night, or at least try to. He told himself not to think about any of that—just to take whatever came—but it was all there, hanging over him.

"What are we supposed to do now?" Yuki heard a man ask.

"Lieutenant Freeman said to stay here for now," someone else answered. Yuki still had his eyes closed.

"That's not what I'm talking about. What do we do without Sergeant Koba?"

But no one answered. They all knew the problem. The lieutenant had the bars on his shoulders, but Sergeant Koba had always known what to do. No one else could lead them into action the way he had done.

"Have you seen Mat?" Shig asked.

Yuki was startled. He sat up. "No. Haven't you seen him?"

"He was with us when we started up the hill, but I haven't seen him since."

Yuki got up quickly and looked around. Men were smoking cigarettes or lying down, mostly quiet now. But he didn't see Mat. "Has anyone seen Sergeant Matsumoto?" he asked.

Sergeant Oshira was sitting on the ground nearby. "No," he said. "But a lot of guys didn't make it up the hill."

Yuki and Shig started walking, not saying a word to each other.

"There's no reason to go looking for him," Oshira said. "The medics will . . ."

But they kept going. They walked straight to a medic about halfway down the hill. He was removing one of the dog tags from the chain around a soldier's neck. Yuki recognized the dead man. Private Saito. The new kid.

Yuki didn't want to do this—didn't want to grieve, didn't want to feel.

"Oh, man," Shig said. "He didn't even have time to get his uniform dirty." And then, after a few seconds: "He ought to be driving a hot rod, chasing girls. He should have had a life."

The medic looked up, nodded, his face grim. He wasn't all that much older himself. Yuki could only think that all of them, all the soldiers strewn across the hill, alive or dead, shouldn't be there, should be home, still being boys. But he didn't say anything, couldn't.

"Did you work on a guy named Matsumoto?" Shig asked the medic.

"I don't know. I don't think so."

"He didn't make it up the hill. So where would he be?"

"Probably at the aid station back toward Bruyères—or at least on his way there. But you're not allowed to go back that far."

Again, Yuki and Shig didn't say anything. They simply continued down the hill. They asked a few people—mostly medics—where the aid station was, and all of them told them the same thing: They shouldn't go there. But they kept going anyway, walked at least a mile, and when they found the station, they asked a staff sergeant—a husky white guy who seemed to be in charge—whether a soldier named Matsumoto was there.

He was walking past them, moving fast. "I don't know. But that's not your concern. Just head back to the line."

Yuki ran after him and grabbed his arm. "We need to know."

The sergeant pulled his arm loose and shouted, "I said, go back to the line!"

"He's our buddy," Shig said.

The sergeant spun around. "Do you think I don't know that? We can't have all you guys hiking down here to see where your friends are. We're trying to patch them up the best we can, but we don't have *visiting hours*."

Yuki stepped closer. "Tell us where to look," he said.

"Watch yourself, Corporal. You're about to get yourself into very big trouble."

Yuki stepped back a little, dropped his head. "I'm sorry," he said. "But please, tell us where we can look for him."

The sergeant pointed. "Over there," he said. "Have your look, and then get out of here."

Yuki and Shig walked in the direction the sergeant had pointed. Yuki could see body bags on the ground, lined up in a row, and he saw some men who were not yet bagged, lying on their backs.

One of them was Mat.

"No," Shig said. He walked closer and then dropped to his knees. "This can't happen."

Yuki wanted to scream, wanted to lie down on the ground and cry, but instead, a kind of disconnection came over him, as though he were floating above himself, only viewing all of this from a distance. He looked down at his friend. He forced himself to draw in air, but he still couldn't make words out of his thoughts, couldn't process what this was going to mean.

There was no sign of a wound. Wherever Mat had been hit, it didn't show. And yet, he didn't look like the same person. His face had flattened like a lump of clay, and his skin looked gray.

Yuki and Shig didn't speak. Yuki knelt down next to Shig, but he didn't touch the body, only stared, tried to find the actual Mat in the thing he was looking at. By then, a reaction was taking shape. What Yuki felt was lost, as though he were no more than clay himself. He knew he couldn't take much more of this.

Shig said, "He never should have come back to the platoon."

"I know." But Yuki remembered what Mat had said. "He came back to look after me."

"It's not your fault, Yuki. He just felt wrong about going home."

The sergeant was back at their side, and Yuki expected him to command them to leave. But the man stood for a time without speaking and then said, "I heard an officer tell one of our medics that your friend carried a soldier off the hill. He got shot in the back but kept going. The soldier he was carrying is still alive. The officer said he was going to write your friend up for a medal."

Some trade, Yuki thought. His life for a ribbon and a little hunk of metal.

"I see this every day," the sergeant said. "We drag these boys down here, shot up or dead. We do what we can for the living, and we process the paperwork for the KIAs. I shouldn't have gotten on you men like that, but you need to understand, I don't want to know who the dead ones are, and I don't want to know their friends. It's better for us down here not to feel too much. Do you understand what I'm saying?"

"Sure," Yuki said, but then he told the sergeant about Mat anyway. "His name was Matsumoto. He was half Japanese, half white. He had a college degree. He could have been an engineer if anyone in the States had been willing to hire him. But half white or not, he was a *Jap* in America, so no one wanted to work with him."

It was not the kind of thing Yuki usually said to white people. But he was tired. He didn't care. He didn't want this sergeant to "process" Mat without knowing the price he had paid.

"I'll tell you the truth," the sergeant said. "I had the same attitude at one time. I'd never been around Japanese people, and I didn't want to be. I don't know what I thought you were like, but I just figured—you know, especially after Pearl Harbor—that you had no business coming over here to fight. As far as I was concerned, the government could keep you in those camps and never let you out."

Yuki looked at the sergeant, actually saw him for the

first time. He was older than most of the soldiers. There was a forlorn quality about him—in his eyes and in the sag of his cheeks—as though all this death and mutilation was sinking deeper into him every day.

"But I'll tell you what," the sergeant continued. "No one in this army fights the way you men do. We've all witnessed it. I've seen regular units get thrown back, and then the Japanese troops go in and get the job done."

"That's why you see so many of us down here at your aid station," Shig said.

"I know. But you're respected by those who know what really goes on over here."

"Maybe the Germans get a lot of us, but we get more of them," Yuki said. He was surprised by his own words, but he didn't want the *Nisei* to be seen only as the soldiers who got shot to pieces. He wanted people to know that the Four-Four-Two was helping to win the war. He wanted this sergeant to say that to people, and not make AJA soldiers out to be fools or fanatics.

"I know that's true too," the sergeant said softly. "And you're not just good soldiers; you're good men." He hesitated a moment, and then added, "Anyway, I just wanted you to know that's how I feel. I see lots of you coming down the way you two did. It's because you look out for each other. I respect that, even if I wish you'd stay away."

"Thank you." Yuki reached out his hand. "My name's Yuki Nakahara. This is Shig Omura."

"Nick Brown," the sergeant said as he shook hands with them.

"We'll go back now," Yuki said. "Take care of him, okay?"

"Yeah. I will."

"Where will he be buried?" Shig asked. "Will they send his body home, or will he be over here somewhere?"

"I can't say for sure. But most likely here."

"And his family will never see him again."

"In all likelihood, they won't."

Yuki had known that, but it had never seemed so important before. Mat's parents were in Hawaii, waiting and hoping, and this son they were so proud of was gone now—just gone. All those pretty sisters he'd talked about would miss their brother for the rest of their lives. They wouldn't even have a chance to bury him.

Yuki turned hard and walked away, and Shig hurried after him. They headed to the hill, back up toward their platoon. "What will the lieutenant do to us?" Shig asked. "You know, for leaving the platoon?"

"I don't care," Yuki said. "If he wants to put me in jail, that would suit me just fine."

"Are you okay, Yuki?"

Yuki didn't answer. He stopped walking, turned around and looked back in the direction of the aid station and Bruyères. The sun was angling across the mountains. The deep green trees were still wet enough to glow in the sunlight. Yuki took long breaths, tried to let some of that beauty and life come into him. But he was feeling nothing. He couldn't even cry. He had never heard of Bruyères until a week ago. He didn't know who lived there. However crucial the site was to military leaders, he had to wonder whether it was worth the terrible cost to take it. He hoped the townspeople felt liberated, not devastated.

Yuki finally turned and looked up the hill, but then the attack all came back to him, the fury he had felt as he had made his charge at the Germans, wanting only to kill.

"I did something," he told Shig.

"What do you mean?"

"I almost shot that German soldier up there in the trees."

"I know."

"He'd been hit, and he was trying to hide, but I almost pulled the trigger anyway, just because I wanted to kill someone."

Yuki wondered what that German soldier with the wound in his head had gone through, what it must have been like to wait at the top of the hill and hear all those banzai shouts, see men wild with anger charging and shooting. Maybe the guy had been a new recruit; maybe he had been terrified. He must have retreated with the others, but then that bullet had gouged out part of his skull. Maybe he hadn't known how bad it was; maybe he'd thought he could hide somehow, and live.

"I aimed at him," Yuki said. "He was looking right at me. There was blood all over him. I almost shot him anyway."

"But you didn't do it."

"At the last second, I saw the look on his face, like he was in agony. But I still wanted to kill him. I wanted to watch his chest blow open and see his blood pour out."

Shig's eyes stayed steady. "We were all crazy mad, and no one would have blamed you if you had shot that guy. But you didn't. That shows what kind of man you are."

"But this whole thing is getting inside me."

"That's not true, Yuki. You're the best man I know. You carried Mat off that hill. What I always know is that if I go down, you won't let me die—not if you can help it."

"And you would do the same for me, Shig. But I don't know what kind of man I'll be if this stuff goes on much longer."

"You'll be who you are, Yuki. You believe in honor. It's deep inside you. You won't let anything get in the way of that."

Yuki tried to think what the word meant. Honor. He had thought he'd known when he had joined the army. Now he only knew that he couldn't let his friends down. He had to fight for them, and he expected them to fight for him. Nations didn't go to war. Men did. Boys did. The trouble was, defending his friends meant killing the boys from some other nation: boys he actually had nothing against. Back in training, he had imagined the Germans he would fight—and they were all brutal Nazis. He had assumed they all hated Jews, hated people of every race but their own, and certainly would think nothing of killing him and his Japanese friends. But the German soldiers he had seen looked about like the boys he had gone to high school with: young, not angry, guys who probably missed their families and wanted to get home just like he did. Maybe they had believed what Hitler told them, had joined the army out of their own sense of duty. And maybe they now hated war as much as he did.

Yuki heard a woodpecker knocking its beak against a tree, the sound reverberating through the forest. He wanted more than anything to go for a walk, look around, see the forest without watching for an enemy behind each tree. It was hard to remember what it was like to let go, to simply enjoy a day.

"Do you believe in heaven?" Shig asked.

Yuki was not at all surprised by the question. But he didn't have an answer ready, so he only asked, "Why?"

"I'm just wondering about Mat."

Yuki knew what his minister back home had said about life after death. There was a heaven, he had said, a place of peace and glory, where a person could be with God. And he knew what his Buddhist father had told him once: that life is a spark that shines brightly for a moment and then goes out of sight, but the spark returns to the earth and is never obliterated. Yuki wasn't sure which of those ideas he believed, or whether he believed either one. But he had seen something, and it was still on his mind. "Mat's body looked like something left behind after his soul—or whatever you call it—went out of him. I don't think life just vanishes. It must continue on in some way."

"That's kind of what I was thinking. Whatever that was down there on the ground, that wasn't Mat."

Yuki nodded. He wanted to believe that. He wanted to believe that death didn't take everything away. Tomorrow he would shoot at people again, and they would shoot at him. He didn't want to think that he was ending *everything* for those men—or that they could end him.

CHAPTER 14

For a week, one furious battle followed another in the mountains of the Vosges Forest. As the 442nd—now reassigned to the Thirty-Sixth Infantry Division, known as the "Texas Division"—pushed to the east, German forces continued to hold the high ground. The *Nisei* soldiers were still segregated from white soldiers, but it was clear to Yuki and his friends that General John Dahlquist, commander of the division, liked to throw the Four-Four-Two into the toughest fights. And the battles were getting more and more intense. With each defeat, German troops retreated closer to the border of their homeland, and they seemed to be fighting ever more urgently.

Two days after Sergeant Koba had been killed, Lieutenant Freeman was shot through the belly and he too was carried from the battlefield. The last anyone had heard, he wasn't dead, but he certainly wouldn't be returning to battle, and no replacement officer had arrived to lead Second Platoon. The men sorrowed over the loss, and the emptiness Yuki had been feeling only deepened. More than half the original platoon was gone, and many of the replacements were already wounded or killed.

A lot of the white officers—platoon leaders and company commanders—had also become casualties, and there simply weren't enough new officers arriving to replace them. Sergeant Oshira had been promoted to platoon sergeant, and rumor had it that he would be receiving a battlefield commission as a second lieutenant. For now, he was leading the men as a sergeant first class. He had always been a strong, smart leader, but he was hardened by battle now, and Yuki hoped the rumors were correct. He didn't want a young lieutenant fresh out of Officer Candidate School to be shipped in to take Lieutenant Freeman's place.

Yuki had been promoted to squad leader and had received his sergeant stripes. Shig had become the fire team leader and a corporal. Yuki had not wanted the rank, and Shig had been even more hesitant, but in the few months they had been in Italy and France, they had learned plenty, and they were some of the most experienced soldiers in their platoon.

Everything was different now. Yuki found himself surrounded by soldiers with little combat experience. They caught on fast if they lasted a battle or two, but Yuki hadn't trained with them, didn't feel connected to them, and he wasn't as confident in their ability as he had been with the "old hands" who made up the original unit.

Yuki also worried that some of the men who had been around the longest were the ones getting most discouraged. One night Yuki and the other squad leaders were called in by Sergeant Oshira to talk over the next day's attack. What Yuki heard sounded like the same old thing: another uphill charge, which could mean another day of heavy losses. The rain had stopped for a while that afternoon, but dark clouds were dropping low again, and rain would probably pelt the soldiers in the night.

After the meeting, Yuki walked back to the foxholes with Sergeant Del Hirinaka. He was one of the last men left from Mat Matsumoto's original squad and he had taken over as squad leader. Days were short now. The sun was already setting, the damp air under the trees filling with a misty brown glow.

Sergeant Hirinaka stopped before they reached the men. He turned and looked at Yuki. "How long can we keep doing this?" he asked. "General Dahlquist just keeps using us for everything that no one else wants to do. I think we're *expendable* to him. He'd rather lose us than the guys in his precious Texas Division."

"I don't want to believe that," Yuki told him. "The Thirty-Sixth was taking a beating before we got here. Those guys have paid a heavy price themselves. And most of them aren't Texans anymore—they're as full of replacements as we are."

"They may not be Texans," Hirinaka said, "but they're *white*. And they still don't want to serve with us."

"But we've won their respect. I don't hear anyone saying that we're disloyal—or that we won't fight."

"They *can't* say that. And we're just fine as long as we keep to ourselves. But General Eisenhower is never going to integrate the troops. When Roosevelt finally made up his mind to send us over here, it was Eisenhower who said he didn't want us."

Yuki knew that. All the AJA troops had heard the story. And the truth was, Yuki didn't see much change in attitude—except in a few individuals. Yuki's mom had written him that home newspapers were making a big deal out of the Japanese American units, reporting all their successes. But she was still reading those newspapers in a prison camp.

Yuki knew something else. It didn't do any good to grouse about that stuff, and the men in his squad couldn't give way to the weariness they were feeling. He was a leader now, and he had to do his best to keep up morale.

"I wouldn't complain so much if I felt better," Hirinaka said. "I'm just sick of living in mud. I don't dare look at my feet, they're so messed up. They get hurting so bad sometimes, I can't think straight."

"I know. Most of us are dealing with the same

problem. General Dahlquist needs to pull us back for a few days and let us dry out—and give the medics time to treat our feet." But admitting to his pain only seemed to make things worse. It was suddenly hard to stand without shifting his weight from one foot to the other.

"We can't keep this up much longer—fighting uphill every day," Hirinaka said. He cursed, with surprising bitterness in his voice. "My men have started talking about wanting to get shot, just to get out of here."

Yuki had heard the same thing. After the day Mat had gone down, Fox Company had been part of a special task force. They had marched at night, looped behind Hill D, and attacked in a pincer movement that had pressed the Germans from both sides. The move had been effective, and a lot of enemy troops had been killed or taken as prisoners, but there had been American casualties too, and the men had lost a night of sleep. Since then they had been on the attack every day, working their way through the woods, taking lots of fire but pushing the Germans back time and again. And every night had been long and cold and wet. Digging new foxholes day after day in ground full of rocks, attacking each morning, seeing more and more of their brothers go down—all of it was a nightmare, and Yuki knew he was reaching a breaking point. He didn't want to leave the battle on a litter, but he understood why some men might consider that an option.

Still, it didn't help to talk about it. Hirinaka seemed to

know that too. "I guess for now we just take one day at a time," he said.

"Yeah. And we can't talk like this in front of our men. Let's get back to them."

Yuki strode out as best he could on his painful feet. When he got back to his squad, he checked on foxholes, asked the men about their feet, and told them they would be attacking at 0800. He didn't hint that he saw anything very difficult in that.

Shig was digging a foxhole. Yuki told him, "Let's not dig too deep. We won't be here long."

"Yeah, well, that's not what you'll say if we take fire tonight." Shig tossed a shovelful of dirt out on the ground. He was only knee-deep so far, and he and Yuki both knew they would have to get deeper, though they were digging where tree roots made the job hard. Shig looked up at Yuki in the dim light. "Are we going after another hill in the morning?" he asked.

"Yeah. We are."

Yuki couldn't see Shig very well in the twilight, especially when he looked down again to dig, but Yuki had caught a glance of something he hated to see. Shig never showed much emotion—especially not discouragement. But he looked broken tonight.

"Get out of there," Yuki told him. "Let me dig for a while."

Shig didn't argue. He stepped out of the hole and sat

down on the wet ground. There was no getting dry anyway, and no way to stay warm at night.

Yuki and Shig took turns digging until Yuki finally said, "That's as deep as we're going to get with that big root blocking the way."

"I'm sure it will be nice to sleep on."

"Who sleeps?"

"I do. That's the only thing I look forward to anymore." But Shig seemed to regret his complaints. His voice softened when he asked, "How bad are your feet, Yuki?"

"Not good. Once I get up and around, they don't hurt so bad, but when I try to sleep, they swell up and the pain gets hard to deal with."

"Let's change your socks." Shig sat up and slipped closer to the hole, let his legs hang inside. He put a hand on Yuki's shoulder. "I'll help you do it."

"I don't know if I dare. I'm afraid if I pull these socks off, all the flesh on the bottom of my feet will come off too."

"You gotta tell someone. You can't keep going on this way."

"Everybody's got bad feet. I'm not going to sit at an aid station and cry about—"

"It's not just 'sore feet.' You could be crippled for life."

Yuki had been thinking the same thing. But he still couldn't ask to leave the line. There were so many new guys who didn't know what they were doing. The experienced men had to run the show and keep the replacements from getting killed. "I'll tell you what," he said. "I've had some stockings inside my shirt for two days. They're pretty dry. Help me put them on, and then I'll help you change yours."

"I'm okay for another day. Let's just get you fixed up for now."

So the two got into the foxhole, which was drier than the surface ground at this point. They sat with their backs against opposite ends, and Shig pulled Yuki's right foot onto his lap. He loosened the laces on the boot, and then he tried to pull it off, but the boot pulled at Yuki's wet stocking and stretched the putrefying flesh. "Stop!" Yuki gasped. "Wait just a minute. Unlace the boot a little more, and then pull easy."

But that didn't work any better.

"I guess you might as well jerk it off all at once," Yuki finally said.

Shig did it, and Yuki didn't scream, but he wanted to. He tried to let the pain calm, but that didn't work, so after a time he said, "Okay, take the sock off carefully. Let's just see what happens."

Shig had to roll the heavy stocking off a little at a time. Yuki wouldn't let himself cry, but tears ran down his cheeks anyway. And once the sock was off, he didn't want to see his foot. He simply asked, "How bad is it?"

"I can't see very well. Some of the skin came off. I can tell that."

"Well, that's not so bad. Let's get a dry sock on and leave the boot off to dry for a little while. We'll do the other foot tomorrow."

"I think we need to change that one too, Yuki."

"Well . . . okay. You're probably right." So they repeated the whole process, and Yuki dealt with the pain again. And then, before they put the wet boots back on, he sat and let his feet air out. Shig held Yuki's ankles, elevated them, and the fresh socks, which were quite dry, soothed the pain a little. Yuki thought of nights when he was a boy and his legs would ache after he'd run around all day. His mother had rubbed his legs and he had loved her tender touch. Shig certainly wasn't his mother, but Yuki's reaction was similar. It was like being home and having someone look after him. He didn't say that to Shig, but as the darkness deepened, Yuki no longer tried to stop his tears. He needed something in his life that wasn't ugly, and Shig's gentleness was almost more than Yuki could bear.

But the boots had to go back on, and all the necessary pushing brought back the pain, which persisted into the night. And the rain came again. Yuki didn't sleep much, despite how weary he was. It was strange to think, after all the battles, all the loss of friends, that this pain in the night seemed the worst of the suffering he had experienced. More than anything, he needed sleep—escape from his days—but these nights lasted longer than any he had ever known.

At first light Yuki was up, glad to move around enough to get his blood flowing. He quietly rousted the soldiers in his squad and told them to eat something. They would be moving out soon. He ate some C rations himself. He had almost no appetite, but he knew that he needed strength.

At exactly 0800, Yuki led his squad through the trees to the bottom of a hill, and then they started their ascent with the rest of their company. They hoped to push forward as far as possible before being spotted or heard. The Germans would be in position near the crest of the hill, and certainly they would be expecting an attack this morning.

The men made little runs from one tree to another. They couldn't see any sign of the enemy ahead, and they hoped they weren't being watched yet, but it was hard to know. The Germans might be letting them get close before they let loose their firepower.

The men moved about three hundred yards up the hill and nothing happened. Yuki used hand signals and his own actions to lead the way. Other squads flanked them on both sides; Hirinaka's men were on the left. Squads from First Platoon were making the same climb not far away. There was no spotting one another in the dense forest, but all the squad leaders had been instructed to move slowly and stealthily until they began to take fire.

Yuki had started to wonder whether the German forces had vacated the area, but then a single sniper bullet snapped through the air. Yuki heard a grunt, a moan, heard a man somewhere in the forest hit the ground. Sniper fire was terrifying; a soldier never knew when the enemy had a scope trained on him.

Yuki ducked behind a tree as soon as the bullet broke the quiet. He could see his seven men, all on their bellies or behind trees. Shig, Ted Tanna, and Yoshi Higa were still in his squad. The other four were replacements, and two of them were engaged in their first battle. Shig was closest, crouched behind a big pine with low-hanging limbs. Yuki knew the men had to keep going, not let a sniper stop them, so he bolted quickly to a tree about twenty yards ahead. Shig did the same, and then his other men made their own runs. Hirinaka's squad was moving up the same way. And then machine-gun fire began to echo in the forest, seeming to bounce from one tree to another.

Yuki saw the muzzle fire and aimed his rifle at it. He pulled off a few rounds, as a lot of men were doing, but the gun was well blockaded with stones and tree limbs. Yuki knew that someone had to get closer and use a grenade, but it would be hard to toss a grenade with so many limbs in the way. He made another move forward and waited for his men to do the same, and then he fired at the machine gun again, but his angle was no better. The worst thing was, Hirinaka's squad was more directly in front of the gun emplacement. If Hirinaka and his men attempted a charge, they would have to run head-on into the fire.

Yuki looked around and waved for Shig to come up to him. Shig made the run and dropped down next to him. "Can you shoot that grenade launcher you've been carrying around?" Yuki asked.

"Sure."

Yuki had his doubts. All the men had been picking up firepower by adopting weapons from men who were knocked out of action. Shig had acquired a rifle with a grenade launcher attached to the barrel, but he had never had a chance to fire it.

"I'm going to get a couple more guys up here, and we're going to lay down cover for you. You move up to where you can see that emplacement and try to knock it out."

"All right. I can do that."

"Don't take chances. Don't run out in the open. Shoot from under the limbs. You won't have to get as close as you would if you had to throw the grenade."

"I know." Shig pointed through the woods. "I'll stay off to this side and then make a run to that big tree. I can shoot from there."

"That looks too close. You better not . . ."

But Shig was on his way, angling right, away from the line of fire and up through the trees. Yuki waved for more of his men to move in closer. "Be ready to put suppressing fire on that emplacement when I give you the signal," he whispered to the men. Then he waited for Shig. But the wait was tedious, and the machine gun was holding the other squads in place. He hoped Hirinaka's squad wouldn't charge before Shig got off a shot.

Yuki watched as Shig made three more little runs and finally reached the tree he had pointed out. As soon as he hit the dirt, he raised up on his elbows, aimed, and fired. But his range was off. The grenade passed over the machine-gun nest and exploded beyond it.

Yuki and his men were pouring cover fire on the emplacement, but the gun was still scattering bullets into the woods. Shig rolled over in the wet leaves under the tree. He grabbed a second grenade and reloaded, but by then Yuki saw bullets thumping into the ground around him.

Shig waited while the entire platoon blasted the emplacement. When the direction of the fire swung back down the hill, Yuki saw Shig roll back to where he could take aim, and he fired a second time. This time his aim was accurate. An explosion rocked the emplacement, and the gun went silent. Yuki broke from behind the tree where he had been waiting, and his men followed him. The other squads made their break at the same time. There were plenty of bullets in the air but no machine-gun fire. The platoon ran up through the woods in an all-out charge.

Yuki expected to run directly into the German line, but at the last moment the Germans began jumping up, retreating, walking backward, continuing to fire. And then they started to turn and run.

The order was to rout the enemy, chase them off the hill, and take over the high ground. That was accomplished. But some of the men chased into the woods, taking out as many Germans as they could. In some ways, that only made sense. More battles were ahead. But Yuki knew the woods were treacherous; even retreating men might find places to hide and set up ambushes. Besides, he felt no zeal to hunt men down.

Now that the position was secure, Yuki looked for Shig. He feared that he had been hit back there under the tree. But as Yuki hurried to the spot, he saw his friend walking toward him, smiling. "Hey, that launcher works," he said.

"You're lucky you got two tries. I'm surprised you didn't get shot after you missed that first time."

"I did get shot."

"What?"

Shig pulled his pack off and showed it to Yuki. A bullet had hit the handle of the "entrenching tool"—his shovel—that was attached to his pack. "Those guys must hate this shovel as much as I do. Why else would they shoot at it?"

Yuki could only think that Shig had come too close one more time. But he was glad to see him smiling, and glad they had survived another charge.

CHAPTER 15

Fox Company finally got pulled off the line. The men took showers and had a chance to dry out in tents. A medic did what he could for Yuki's feet. He soaked them in a solution that stung, put some dry socks on him, and then told Yuki to rest and not put his boots on. The boots, above all, needed to dry, and his feet needed air. The medic also gave Yuki an aspirin tablet, which didn't really take the pain away, but at least Yuki felt better knowing that he wasn't doing anything to make things worse. The rain had let up somewhat, but the temperature was steadily dropping, and even in the tent, Yuki felt the cold.

The men hoped for a long rest. They stayed in their tents most of the time, kept as warm as they could, and slept.

Yuki needed that, but he didn't like the sound of a rumor that was going around. Word was circulating that the First Battalion of the 141st Infantry Regiment—some of the Texas Division soldiers—had pushed too far into the Vosges Forest and had gotten cut off and surrounded by German forces. All the talk—mostly whispered by officers to sergeants and then on to enlisted men—was that General Dahlquist had refused to listen to intelligence officers who reported to him that German troops still occupied the area. After the First Battalion was cut off, the two other battalions of the 141st had tried several times to break through the German lines to rescue the surrounded soldiers, but each attempt had failed. Supplies had been air-dropped to the stranded men, but most of those parachutes had missed their target, and the men were running out of food and ammunition.

The predicament of the cut-off battalion was the main subject of discussion in the camp—and something to gripe about. Soldiers were always skeptical about high-ranking officers who moved troops around without knowing the actual situation up front. Yuki wondered whether the general would learn from his mistake. He didn't like the thought of being commanded by someone too proud to listen to his advisers.

Yuki was resting in his tent when Sergeant Oshira came to talk to him. The sergeant stood by Yuki's cot, but he looked at the tent wall, not at Yuki. "I gotta tell you something you won't want to hear," he said.

"We must be going back to the line."

"Yeah. But it's worse than that. They've ordered us to break through to that cut-off battalion."

"You can't be serious."

"I wish I weren't."

"When do we go?"

"We move out this afternoon. We go into battle in the morning."

Yuki felt as though Sergeant Oshira had stepped on his chest and forced all the air out of him. He wondered whether he had the strength to get up, let alone to walk on his painful feet. But he didn't say that to the sergeant. He knew he had to make himself do it, however impossible it seemed at the moment. Still, he couldn't hide his frustration when he said, "Are we really the only troops they can send in there?"

Sergeant Oshira shut his eyes, took a breath. "Yuki," he said, "I'm not going to say this to anyone else, but I need to say it to someone. What they're doing to us is wrong. We get all the worst assignments. You know exactly what the general is thinking: That the *Nisei* troops will sacrifice half their men again, but they won't stop, no matter what."

Neither said anything for a time. Yuki's initial rage was dying quickly, and a grim sense of inevitability was taking over.

"I guess it's what we asked for," Sergeant Oshira said. "We told the army we wanted a chance to prove ourselves. The trouble is, I'm not sure anyone's paying attention to what we've done."

"*We* know."

"Sure, we do. But headquarters promised us some time off because we *need* it, and now the general is going back on his word." He ducked his head for a moment. "But you know what? We can complain all we want—we still have to get our men ready to go."

Yuki sat up. "Can you help me get my boots on?" he asked.

"Rest for a while longer. We still have a few hours before we move out."

"But I need to start moving around. And I want to be the one to break the news to my squad. I have to say the right things so they don't go in feeling sorry for themselves."

"I guess that's right. We also need to start by getting our own heads ready."

Sergeant Oshira picked up Yuki's boots and stepped to the end of the cot. Pushing the boots on was an even worse ordeal than when Shig had helped. It was all Yuki could do not to scream. By the time the boots were back on, he was out of breath, and the pain seemed to fill his whole body.

"Don't get up yet," Sergeant Oshira told Yuki. "Let your feet get used to the boots."

Yuki knew that was not really going to happen, but he wasn't ready to put his weight on his feet just yet.

"Maybe you can't do this, Yuki," the sergeant said. "Just say the word and I'll get an ambulance in here to take you to an aid station."

"No." Yuki didn't explain. He just hoped the pain would gradually calm.

Sergeant Oshira stood by him as though he were considering whether to overrule Yuki's judgment. After a couple of minutes, Yuki realized he had to sit up to convince the man that he could do what he had to do.

But when the sergeant turned to go, Yuki said, "When's our luck going to run out, Sarge? I keep thinking, there's no way I can keep surviving these battles."

"I don't let myself think about that. A while back I realized, I'll probably get killed sooner or later. So I just take that attitude every time we go after another hill. And I'm okay with that. I'll die, if that's what it takes. I just think we should be looked at as *assets*, not throwaways. That's the only thing I'm complaining about."

"That's how we all feel." Yuki extended his hand. "Help me up. I need to walk." So Sergeant Oshira grabbed Yuki's hand and raised him up slowly. Yuki tried not to let the pain show in his face.

"Are you sure, Yuki? Can you do this?"

"Yeah. I'll manage."

"I appreciate it. I really need you, Sergeant."

The two stood and looked at each other for a moment. Here they were, both noncommissioned officers, both "men of experience" after less than five months at the battlefront. They had shipped out together, fought every battle together, but it was Oshira, when he was squad leader, who had taught Yuki most of what he knew about the realities of actual war. Yuki had watched the man put his life on the line for his men, over and over, and it was what Yuki knew he had to do now.

"When you say you figure you'll die," Yuki said, "don't you think about your family back home?"

"Sure I do. At least I'm not married, like some of the guys. But I have a brother who's training at Camp Shelby right now, and if we both go down, I don't know what that would do to my parents." He looked past Yuki, seemed to be considering, as though he were trying to imagine that kind of future for his parents. "I'm not saying that I want to give up my life. I'm just saying it's what might happen and I can't do very much about it."

"I thought I knew that when I came over here, but I didn't. Not really."

"Sure. That's how it is."

Yuki was still breathing steadily, still trying to allow the pain to abate, and trying to convince himself that he needed to stay with his unit, even though he had a good excuse to go back to an aid station and get more rest.

"Here's what I've been thinking," Yuki said. "My father never talked to me much, but he told me about *bushido*—the way of the samurai. He called it 'honor to the death.' He told me that a man of honor never shames his family. He fights to preserve what is right and good. We don't like to say things like that now because we don't want to admit how Japanese we still are, but I think it's why we fight so hard, why we win our battles. We believe in honor."

"I don't know, Yuki. I didn't hear much about that kind of stuff in my house. We didn't keep to the old ways."

"But those attitudes came down to you anyway. It's just in us. When I was a kid, the only thing I wanted was to be an *American*—like all the other kids. I was ashamed that my father was so Japanese and couldn't speak English. But I don't feel that way now. I don't think we should try to run away from who we are."

"Here's the thing, Yuki. When you go home, you'll be a Jap again, not a warrior. No one's going to give you credit for your *honor*."

Yuki didn't want to believe that, but he knew it might be true. "Maybe they never will respect us, no matter what we do. But I'll respect myself. And that's what I've always needed to do."

Sergeant Oshira nodded, and the two took another long look at one another. "Whatever we call it, I know we'll go after those guys that are trapped up there in the mountains, and if they can be reached, we'll reach them."

It was Yuki's turn to nod. And then he followed Sergeant Oshira from the tent, hobbling along as best he could. He talked to his men, tried not to deny them their own anger—and didn't say a word about honor. He only let them know that they were needed again.

Yuki learned from Sergeant Oshira later in the day that the 100th Battalion, along with Third Battalion of the 442nd, would make the head-on assault. Second Battalion, including F Company, would attempt to take the high ground on a hill designated as 617. This would give them a position above the stranded battalion. The frontal attack would probably be the worst, but Hill 617 was heavily fortified and a tough objective.

Winter gear had still not reached the troops and the colder weather was tough to deal with. But late in the day, as the men began their trudge back into the mountains, Yuki found the cold didn't bother him as long as he kept moving. His feet were the real problem. He didn't want to limp, didn't want to put any doubt about his readiness in the minds of his squad, so he kept up and tried not to let his pain show.

When he fell in next to a young private, newly arrived from the States, he wondered how scared the boy was. "Where you from, Fujioka?" he asked the soldier.

"Southern Cal," Fujioka said, and he sounded like any other California kid.

"Were you in an internment camp?"

"Yeah. I was in Manzanar, up by the Sierra Nevada. I

got drafted from there." That was one big change in what was happening back in the States—Japanese Americans were now subject to the draft the same as anyone else, even though their families were still being held in camps.

"Are you feeling okay so far?"

Fujioka looked over at him. He was a lean, muscular young man, good-looking. He walked like an athlete, with a certain looseness and confidence. "Sure," he said. "You don't have to worry about me. I'll hold up my end of the deal."

"Good. I think you will. But you need to know, the first time bullets start whipping through the air, you'll find yourself wanting to dig your way into the ground and just stay there."

"No, I won't be like that. Don't worry." His voice, his nod, his straight shoulders—all said that he was ready for action, but Yuki knew the man was scared. The fact was, he couldn't be much younger than Yuki—a year at most— but the gap between them seemed decades. Yuki felt more than tired, more than hurt; he felt worn down, old.

"You got a girl waiting for you back home?"

Fujioka grinned. "One girl? What are you talking about? More like a dozen."

"So what were you? The local Romeo?"

"What can I say? I got that certain somethin'. No doubt about that."

"And you're a good dancer, right?"

"You know it. Best in my high school."

He was still smiling. Yuki sort of liked the guy. And hated him too. "You know what you are?" Yuki asked.

"What's that?"

"You're me. You're the guy I was when I left the Topaz camp in Utah a year and a half ago."

Fujioka slapped Yuki on the shoulder as though Yuki had no sergeant stripes there, and he said, "Thanks. I guess you mean that as a compliment."

Yuki hated the pride he saw in the replacements. They seemed like Japanese kids trying too hard to act "American." But Yuki told himself that a lot of that cockiness would be gone in a few days.

"Let me tell you a couple of things, Private."

"I'm all ears, Sarge."

"Stay close to me tomorrow and do what I do. When we start an attack, we don't back off, but we move quickly from cover to cover, and we lay down a field of fire to protect each other."

"I know. We learned all that in our training."

Yuki continued to walk alongside Fujioka for maybe another hundred yards. All the while, his anger was mounting. He saw what was coming; he had seen it before. But he wanted to stop it this time. In a quiet voice, he said, "You're going to die tomorrow, Fujioka. Are you ready for that?"

Fujioka stopped, turned toward Yuki. "What?"

"We had another cocky kid join our company a couple

of weeks ago. He's already dead. That's what I expect will happen to you."

"Hey, I'm just saying I'm no coward."

"But you think you know what you're doing and you don't. You think that nothing could ever happen to you because you're God's gift to the world—and you're not. If you're lucky, you'll only get wounded and they'll carry you back to some aid station, where you can remember this conversation. But my guess is, this time tomorrow, your body will be in a bag and they'll be hauling it off to dump in some burial ground your parents will never see."

Fujioka stared at Yuki. Men were streaming around them, but Yuki didn't move on. "I didn't say I know everything, Sergeant. I just—"

"You just think you have to sound tough. But I'm telling you, if you want to live, follow what I do. I'll try to keep you alive."

Fujioka nodded. "Okay."

"I was just as sure of myself as you are when I left home. I told my friends I was going to come home with my chest covered in medals. But I panicked my first day out. I forgot everything I'd been taught. Do you understand what I'm telling you?"

"Yes."

Yuki turned and fell back into stride with the other men in the company. His feet were hurting even more. Fujioka walked next to him, now quiet.

The men kept marching, and that night, in spite of their exhaustion, they dug foxholes again. Once Yuki and Shig were finished, Yuki checked with the other men in his squad. Fujioka and his partner, a replacement named Endo, were still digging, as though they wanted to show that they were trying to do things right.

"I didn't mean to be so tough on you," Yuki said.

"No, it's all right. I deserved everything you said."

"Well, most of it. But mainly, I wanted to get your attention."

"You did."

"All right. That hole is deep enough. Try to get some sleep."

Yoshi Higa was a corporal now and was the other fire team leader along with Shig. Yoshi and Ted Tanna had finished their foxhole and were already bundling up for the night as best they could. Two more replacements, Private Hamada and a half-Japanese boy named Cutler, were still digging. Yuki offered them the same advice: They should watch what the others did and take no wild chances. He then walked back to Shig, and when they got into their hole, they huddled together.

"This one is going to be bad," Shig said.

"The night? Or the battle tomorrow?"

"I was thinking about the night ahead of us. But tomorrow's going to be worse."

Yuki lay quiet for a time, tried to find a position that

wasn't entirely uncomfortable. His feet were throbbing. "How long have we been over here, Shig?" he asked. "Ten years?"

"It seems like it, doesn't it? It's hard to remember any other life."

"Am I the same guy I was when we came over?"

"Yeah, you're still the same guy on the inside. You've just dropped some of the attitude you carried around. What about me?"

"You've always been steadier than I am, Shig. But you're a soldier now. As good as anyone in the whole regiment."

"That's not true. I just try to stay alive."

"But you look out for everybody else, too."

"That's what we all do."

"Well . . . let's keep each other alive again tomorrow."

"Okay."

But Yuki couldn't fight off the feeling that his time was running out.

CHAPTER 16

Before Fox Company joined the assault on Hill 617, Sergeant Oshira offered Yuki some final instructions and then handed him a Thompson submachine gun with four drums of ammo. "I thought you might want to carry this today," he said.

"Where'd you get it?"

"It doesn't matter. We need all the firepower we can get. I figure you're the best guy to handle it." Yuki was pleased. He had fired Thompsons—"Tommy guns," as they were called—and he knew what they could do. He was also pretty sure it was the same gun Sergeant Koba had once used. He liked the idea of carrying forward what the sergeant had done for the platoon, being the kind of leader he had been. But Sergeant Oshira added, "Don't think you're Superman just because you've got a machine gun. You still need to watch yourself."

"Sure. I will." Yuki liked the way the weapon felt in his hands, and he did feel powerful. But he was nervous—more than usual. He had more to be concerned about these days, with men to lead—and men to keep alive.

It was early, still dark. Fog was hanging in the trees, reducing what little visibility Yuki had. It seemed a morning to curl up somewhere warm and sleep as long as possible, not to shatter the peace of the forest.

"Forget what I said yesterday, all right?" Sergeant Oshira said.

"Everything you said was true."

"But it doesn't help us. Let's just do the job. No matter what else is going on, we do have to win this war. We might as well be proud we're the right guys to do it."

"See, Sarge, you do believe in honor."

"What I believe is that we have to drive the Krauts off that hill in front of us. I'm not going to worry about anything else."

The troops set off into the dark and then began their climb up the mountain. Yuki's feet were still burning with pain, but there were too many other things on his mind to allow him to fret about that. Second Platoon—Oshira's men—had the company's lead position, straight up the middle, with the other platoons spread across the base of the mountain. The first light was not penetrating through the tree cover yet, and movement in the dense forest was tricky, but the regimental officers had wanted to get troops up the hill as far as possible before daylight.

Yuki had talked to the men in his squad before they set out. He whispered to them to be as quiet as they could and to keep their equipment from clanking. But that soon became impossible. Yuki heard whispers as the soldiers tried to keep track of one another, and somewhere in the dark a soldier fell and apparently banged his rifle against a tree. Soon after that a mortar shell crashed into the forest, and then more followed. Yuki knew it would be hard for his new men not to panic in the dark when explosions were flashing around them.

"Fujioka," he whispered. "Where are you?"

"I'm right behind you, Sergeant."

"Good. Stay with me."

Then a voice stabbed through the woods. "Stay down until we get some light." It was Sergeant Oshira, who had told Yuki from the beginning that moving through the forest in the dark was never going to work. "One more stupid idea from headquarters," he had called it.

Yuki told his men to hunker down and wait, and he asked each member of his squad to call back to him, but he didn't bring them in any closer. They needed to remain spread out.

It wasn't long before big artillery guns began to fire and trees began to burst. The explosions flung splintered limbs in all directions. Shrapnel cracked through the trees and pounded into the ground. Yuki didn't like anything about this. There was no time to dig in, and it was suicide to sit tight much longer. But after only a few minutes, the barrage stopped. Yuki wasn't sure why. Maybe the Germans were conserving ammunition until they had a target they could clearly identify.

The light was gradually coming, and when the misty air around Yuki turned silver, he knew it was time to push forward, before the shelling started again. Sergeant Oshira was obviously thinking the same thing. He called out, "Second Platoon, move out."

Yuki looked at Shig, who was nearby, on his right.

Shig nodded.

"Let's go," Yuki whispered to his men. Instantly, everyone was up and moving. They worked their way carefully through the trees, walked hard, and for twenty minutes or so met no resistance. But the terrain soon changed. The Germans had chosen a position at the top of a steep, rocky incline. Trees were thinner on the slope, which would make cover harder to find. Yuki had no doubt that the Germans were ready and waiting for the *Nisei* to attempt that dangerous ascent. The trouble was, there was no other way to get to the line of resistance. The platoon had to make it up the mountain as fast as possible, and the entire company had to find angles to shoot through the trees and lay down a shield of suppressing fire on the German weapons.

As soon as the men began the uphill push, overlapping fire from German automatic weapons scattered bullets down through the trees onto the platoon. Yuki found it difficult to make the climb and fire the Thompson at the same time, so he worked his way forward in short bursts, found what cover he could behind a tree or boulder, and then, holding the machine gun waist high, fired in the direction of the gun directly above him. As he fired, his men rushed forward and found cover, then fired their own weapons. Mortar teams were also firing at the German emplacements, and that was slowing their machine guns a little.

Yuki made another run ahead, tried to take cover behind a spindly young tree, but knew he was in a bad spot. He fired his Tommy gun and realized the angle was too steep. All the while, he was hearing bullets batter the rocky slope around him. He made a quick run at a more substantial tree to his left, but now he was trapped. He had outrun his men, and they were taking heavy fire in spite of all the bullets and mortars directed at the German emplacements.

The squad had to either make a dash up the steep face of the mountain or fall back. There were no other options. But Shig made a decision before Yuki could wave him away. He jumped up and ran to Yuki, and the other men followed, all of them angling toward a little copse of trees near Yuki. Shig dropped down next to Yuki, rolled onto his side, and clicked a grenade into place on his launcher.

"No! You can't hit them from here," Yuki said, but Shig was already jumping up. He aimed and fired, but the grenade struck a tree limb and fell far short.

Yuki grabbed at Shig, tried to pull him down. But just as the grenade exploded, Yuki heard two quick thumps, and Shig collapsed to the ground. Yuki grabbed Shig, pulled him behind the tree. "Where are you hit?"

Shig didn't answer. He moaned, sort of whimpered. Yuki rolled Shig onto his back and pulled his jacket open, but as he did, he saw that the two bullets had ripped a wide hole in his gut. Blood was pumping, bubbling through his shirt. Yuki slapped his hand against the wound, tried to hold the blood in. "You're okay, Shig," he pleaded. "We'll get you through this."

But it wasn't true and Yuki knew it.

"Talk to me, Shig. Can you hear me?"

No answer. Shig's eyes were open but he was seeing nothing.

Blood was running between Yuki's fingers and spreading across Shig's shirt. Yuki couldn't think what else to do. "Medic!" he called out, but that was futile. Medics couldn't run into this much fire.

Shig gave a deep gasp, and then all the air seeped out of him. His muscles went limp, his face sagged. "Shig! Don't do this," Yuki was begging. "You can't do this." He slammed his fist against his chest, tried to yell into his face, "Shig, come back to me right now!" but he choked on a sob. He dropped his chin to his chest, said what might have been a prayer: "Please, don't let him die."

But even as he was saying the words, he knew he had seven more men out there taking fire. He had to lead them, had to cover for them.

Yuki took a big breath, fought to control his emotions, and then grabbed the Thompson submachine gun in his bloody hands. He jumped up and charged ahead, then stopped and fired, but he didn't wait for his men this time. He jerked an ammo drum from his weapon and slammed another one in, all the while standing in the open. He had to get up that hill and toss a grenade into that emplacement. He charged off to his right, dropped down, blasted the machine-gun nest with another burst of fire. Then he broke to his left, with bullets popping past his ears. He stopped long enough to fire another burst, and then he ran to his right one more time and dropped behind a tree. He heard the enemy fire let up a little, so he made one more run to his left and one more to his right, found cover once again, and then pulled a grenade from his belt. He took another breath, gathered himself, and then ran straight at the machine gun, climbing frantically over the rocky ground, ripping his fingers, bashing his knees against the rocks.

He stopped, pulled the pin from the grenade, and set his feet. He was still far from his target, so he didn't lob the grenade, but threw it like a baseball. As it left his hand, he felt something strike his chest. It was like a punch, and it sent him spinning backward. A second slam hit him in the shoulder, knocked him off his feet.

After he crashed against the rocky ground, he tried to breathe but couldn't. The tree limbs above him seemed to be spinning. He sucked for air, tried to keep himself alive, but his thought was, *My time has come*. He lay on the ground on his back, and he tried to see the sky, see something. But everything was fading.

"Shig," he said. He stretched his arm out, reached for him, but couldn't find him. He let his eyes go shut, wondered why he didn't feel any more pain than he did, wondered what would come next.

But then someone was there, pulling his jacket open, asking questions. Yuki only heard the voice like a buzzing, couldn't grasp the words. But he knew that time had passed, that he had been on the ground for a while. He wondered what had happened to his men.

Yuki was losing the light again, and that didn't frighten him the way he had always thought it would. But he did think of his mother. She hadn't wanted him to join the army. She hadn't wanted to lose him. He was sorry for that. And Keiko—he had wanted to see her again.

Yuki woke up slowly, his thoughts confused. He was in a tent. At first, he could see the canvas, knew it wasn't sky, and then he realized there were two men—medics—leaning over him, one on each side. They were doing something to his chest. He felt no pain, felt disconnected. He had accepted death, and that acceptance had relieved him. Now he didn't know what would happen to him.

"Sergeant Nakahara, can you hear me?"

Yuki wanted to answer but couldn't. He thought maybe he nodded his head.

"You are *not* going to die. Don't let yourself think that. You've got a collapsed lung, but that won't kill you. You got hit twice and we're not sure what the bullets did to you inside, but we're pumping plasma into you and you're stabilizing. We'll get you to a hospital."

There were times after that when Yuki slept, and times when he was partly awake. Sometimes people talked to him, and he thought he understood some of what they said. But he wasn't certain of anything. He only knew that a kind of haziness—a cloud, it seemed—was filling his head, and it made him want more than anything to sleep.

Yuki awoke once long enough to recognize that he was in the back of some sort of vehicle, and eventually he understood that he had been transported to a hospital in Belmont, not far from Bruyères, and that he had had surgery. But as his mind became clearer, he felt more pain in his chest and shoulder and back. A nurse who spoke little English and who seemed rather oblivious to his pain was in and out of the room where his bed was—a room full of beds and men. He heard talking at times. For a couple more days, Yuki slept most of the time and fought hard to understand his situation whenever he awoke.

But one morning he woke to more clarity than he had known since all this had started, and it was then that he began to remember.

Shig was dead.

Yuki had tried many times to prepare himself for whatever might happen, for the fact that he himself might die, but he had always hoped that Shig would get through. Yuki had pushed forward after Mat had died, mainly by refusing to think about him, but this loss was like a chasm opening up before him. There was no going around it, no plunging through it.

And Yuki knew the worst: He had talked Shig into joining the army. He was responsible for everything his friend had suffered in Italy and France, and now, for his death. He would face Shig's parents someday, and Keiko. He had no idea what he could say to them.

Tears began to seep from the corners of Yuki's eyes. He knew he would never be as close to anyone again. He feared his life now more than he had feared his death. Maybe the army would repair him and send him back to the battle and he could lose himself in the war all over again. But what if the doctors sent him home? He would always know: He hadn't kept Shig alive the way he had vowed to do.

It was all too much. He didn't want to draw attention to himself with other men around, so he pulled his pillow over his face to muffle the sounds, and he let himself cry. "I'm sorry. I'm sorry," he kept saying, but he didn't know whether Shig could hear him. The two of them had talked about life after death, but Yuki wasn't sure about it. Now he wanted to believe. He wanted to see Shig at least one more time, find a way to thank him and tell him face-to-face how sorry he was.

All Yuki could think to do was to pray for Shig to whatever god there might be. He simply asked that Shig would be all right. He repeated the prayer over and over, never stopped, even when he slipped back into the half sleep that overtook him again.

Later in the morning the nurse was there, the Frenchwoman with her black hair tied up behind her head. "You awake?"

Yuki nodded.

"Say it."

"Yes."

"That is good. Someone here to see you."

Yuki raised his head enough to see the man standing behind the nurse. Sergeant Oshira.

"Sarge," he tried to say, but his voice was hoarse and it pinched off.

Sergeant Oshira walked to his bed. Yuki could see that he had a bathrobe on, not a uniform. One arm was inside his robe, making a bulge. "I got hit on the same hill," he said.

"Are you okay?"

"Better than you. My elbow is a mess, probably always will be, but I haven't gone through all the stuff you have."

"Did we . . ." Yuki had to stop to breathe. "Did we take that hill?"

"Yeah. It took us two days, and we lost a lot of men, but we made it. I got hit on the second day. Machine-gun fire, same as you. Guys say it's a million-dollar wound, but that's not what I'm feeling right now. I'd rather finish the job we started."

Yuki felt some of that, but the sergeant sounded as though he still had energy, and the thought of going back to the battle seemed beyond Yuki's strength.

"Shig's dead," Yuki said.

Sarge nodded, then looked down. After a time, he said, "I'm sorry, Yuki."

"War," Yuki said. He didn't know how to say what he was thinking.

"It isn't what we thought it would be, is it?" the sergeant said. He stood for a long time, now looking across the room, but not at the other beds, the other men. He seemed to be seeing through the walls. Finally he added, "We all grow up wanting to be war heroes. What a joke that is."

The absurdity of it all had been pressing into Yuki's mind since that first battle back in Italy, but now, as though he were waking up for the first time in his life, he thought he could see more clearly: People—the ones back home—loved war, no matter what they said. They loved to hear the bands play and see the flag wave. That's why war never stopped. Why couldn't they understand what they were cheering for? Shig was dead.

"Our Four-Four-Two boys got through to that cut-off battalion," Sergeant Oshira said. "We saved more than two hundred lives."

Yuki nodded. He needed to believe that what they had done in the Vosges Forest had had a purpose.

"The trouble is, our regiment lost a lot more than the two hundred we saved."

"How many?"

"More than eight hundred casualties. I don't know how many of that number were killed."

"Eight hundred of us went down saving two hundred?"

"Sure. That's a fair deal. Four of us for each 'true American.' The generals probably figure that's a good trade-off."

"What about my squad? How many of them?"

"I'm not really sure, Yuki. Some were wounded. I don't think anyone was killed—except for Shig."

"What about Fujioka?"

"He was okay the last time I saw him. But he wasn't acting like a big shot."

Yuki nodded. He was relieved to know his prediction for Fujioka hadn't come true. Maybe he had said the right words to him.

"But here's the thing," Sergeant Oshira said. "That grenade you tossed did hit home. It knocked out that machine gun. Your guys were in big trouble. You saved their lives."

That was good. But eight hundred casualties—it was unthinkable. "We had to do it, didn't we, Sarge?"

"Someone did. We don't abandon our own men, no matter what."

That was how Yuki wanted to think about it. He didn't want to think about AJA soldiers saving white soldiers; he wanted to think of brothers saving brothers. "It's something we can be proud of, Sarge. It's what we had to do."

"Yeah, I guess so. But the *Stars and Stripes* just came out with a story about the gallant soldiers who saved the 'Lost Battalion'—that's what they're calling them now. The only photograph they used was the smiling mug of some white soldier. The article never mentioned that it was the 442nd that broke through to save those guys."

Yuki felt the insult, but he told Sergeant Oshira, "We can't worry about that. We know what we did."

"Yeah, I guess."

"Are you going to be okay?"

"No. Not really. This elbow never will work right, they tell me. My feet are getting better, but they're going to be a problem too. Still, I get to have a life. You do too. A lot of our friends gave up *everything*. So I'm not going to complain too much."

Yuki knew that his own body would take a long time to feel right. Along with the new wounds, his feet still hurt, and he had some scars on his face and a slice taken out of his arm. But none of that really mattered to him. He didn't want to feel sorry for himself either, but he had the feeling that nothing was left of him, that he had been killed out on Hill 617, and that for the rest of his life he would have to pretend he was still the kid named Yuki who had joined the army.

After the sergeant left the room, Yuki tried to tell himself that he would simply have to find a way to feel better in time. But he couldn't think past Shig. He kept seeing Shig lying on his back, his face blank. And he saw his own hands pressed against the gaping wound, blood pumping between his fingers and flowing across his shirt. He tightened his eyes, tried not to see that image, but blood seemed to be flowing everywhere, filling up his vision, spreading across everything.

CHAPTER 17

Yuki was still in the army hospital in Belmont, but he was getting up each day, moving around pretty well. He simply had no stamina. Part of his problem was that he wasn't sleeping well. His brain had stored up all the things he had seen in the last six months and was now running all those scenes back through his dreams. What he saw was chaotic: explosions; bodies cartwheeling like acrobats; blood dripping, running, coating his hands. And often he would see the young German boy, or someone similar, lying on his side like a child sleeping.

Noises filled his head too, and not only woke him but scared him. There were times when he curled up and waited for the next shell to drop, or even thought a shell had burst very near, next to his bed. Yuki knew that nurses sometimes discovered him shaking and mumbling and surely told the doctors, who came to his room and asked him whether he was "managing all right." He would tell them that he was fine or admit that he had only had a bad dream. He knew—and surely they knew—that he wasn't fine, but no one forced the issue, and Yuki kept telling himself he would be all right before much longer.

Sometimes Yuki tried to envision his future, to figure out what he wanted to do when he got back to civilian life. But he still couldn't see anything in front of him. He could only remember. Word had gotten around to him that the Four-Four-Two had been pulled out of the Vosges Forest and had been sent to a place called La Houssière. He fantasized about walking from the hospital, going AWOL, and finding a train that would take him back to the men of Fox Company. He knew they were getting some rest, and he longed to be with them. But he also knew that the war wasn't over for those guys, and he wondered how many more of them would die.

In December, the Germans made a desperate attempt to strike back against the Allies. German forces drove hard across the border into Belgium and momentarily routed American and British units in the Ardennes forest. For a time, the front line of battle bulged toward the west; the outbreak was being called the "Battle of the Bulge." But after about three weeks, the Allies defeated the Germans and pushed them back, and from all Yuki was hearing, the German resistance was breaking down.

Yuki couldn't imagine himself in battle again, but

in January, as his strength was returning, he began to ask his doctors whether he could or would be returned to his unit. "No, Sergeant," one doctor finally told him. "The war is winding down in Europe. You won't be well enough in time to go back."

"But what about Japan?"

The army doctor was a lean young man with reddish hair. He looked like he ought to be a schoolboy, not a soldier. He peered through his wire-rimmed glasses, and Yuki knew exactly what he was thinking: *They wouldn't send you to fight the Japanese.* But the doc didn't say that. He said, "I think, in time, you'll be just fine. But when a bullet passes through your chest like that, and damages so many muscles and ribs, it takes a long time to heal entirely. The army will continue to take care of you for a few more weeks—until they think you're well enough— and then you'll get your honorable discharge."

Yuki accepted that. He thought of saying that he would rather go back to the war, but he knew he didn't really want that, and he decided not to make such claims.

Sergeant Oshira came by often and the two shared the rumors they heard. They talked about going home, but they rarely said anything about the battles they had fought together. Then one day, Sergeant Oshira showed up in Yuki's ward with another man, a colonel. He was a stout, studious-looking man wearing a Class A uniform, his hat tucked under his arm. He seemed to be a desk jockey, not a warrior. Sergeant Oshira introduced him as Colonel Orton.

The colonel didn't chat, didn't ask Yuki how he was feeling. He merely said, sounding formal, "Sergeant Nakahara, you have been awarded the Purple Heart medal for the wound you received."

Yuki didn't smile, but he thought it was silly to make a big deal out of a Purple Heart. It seemed as though most of the *Nisei* soldiers had at least one. It was no great achievement to get shot or to catch a piece of shrapnel.

"In addition," the colonel said, "you have been awarded the Silver Star Medal for gallantry in action. I've been asked to make the presentation here, since you won't be returning to your unit."

Yuki was astonished. He stared at the man. "Why?" he asked.

"Why were you awarded a Silver Star?"

"Yes."

"I'll read the official statement, and that should answer your question." He pulled an envelope from the inner pocket of his tunic, extracted a sheet of paper, and read a paragraph about Yuki's bravery under fire in racing up Hill 617 and risking his own life to eliminate an enemy machine-gun emplacement, "saving the lives of many of his fellow soldiers by his actions."

When he had finished, Yuki could think of nothing to say. He glanced toward the other beds in the room and saw that some of the patients had been listening. He didn't want that. Every guy in the ward probably deserved a medal as much as he did.

"I won't pin these medals on you, since you're not in uniform, but you should wear both of them on your uniform when you are ready to travel."

"I'll make sure he does," Sergeant Oshira said.

"But it's a mistake," Yuki said. "We all knocked out machine-gun nests at different times. It's what we had to do."

"That may be true," Colonel Orton said. "But your company commander felt that you went beyond the call of duty. According to him, this was just one example of the way you led and protected your men. Early on, for instance, you carried one man off the field of battle under heavy artillery fire."

But that was Mat, his friend. Did people still not understand that? Yuki looked at Sergeant Oshira. "You wrote me up for this medal, didn't you?"

"I may have started the ball rolling, but everyone in our company agreed that you deserve the honor."

"How can I wear a Silver Star for doing the same sorts of—"

"Sergeant, stop right there," the colonel said. "You might be right. Maybe other soldiers are also deserving, but when you're honored this way, you also represent what the men of your unit achieved."

Yuki was thinking of all kinds of things he could

say—about war, and about bravery—but he decided to let it go. He just wasn't sure he would ever put that medal on his uniform. Still, he took the little box Colonel Orton handed him and opened it. It was a gold five-point star suspended from a ribbon with vertical red, white, and blue stripes. In the middle of the gold star was a small silver one. Yuki had once dreamed of receiving such an honor, and he was not unappreciative of having it now, but he made up his mind quickly: He would take it home, put it away, and remember that his leaders thought him worthy of it—but he would never brag about it, never mention it to anyone.

Two weeks later, Yuki was preparing to be driven to the south of France, and from there, to fly back to the United States. He had dressed in his uniform for the first time since leaving the battlefield. Sergeant Oshira came to visit him again. "Let me pin those medals on you," he told Yuki.

"No. I'm just going to—"

"You need to wear them, Yuki. For all of us in the Four-Four-Two. It's what people back home can understand. They need to know that we fought for our country and we gave it our best."

So Yuki let the sergeant pin the medals on his jacket. He just wasn't sure how long he would leave them on.

"And I'll tell you something else. You *are* brave. You fought as courageously as any man I know."

"I don't know what that means, Sarge. They killed Shig. And the rest of us were in trouble. I had to do something."

"I know, Yuki. I get that. But you didn't curl up and hide. You thought of your men, saw what you had to do, and you did it."

Yuki flew to Washington, D.C., where he entered the Walter Reed General Hospital. He was checked over, processed, and told he needed to rest for a while before the long train trip across the country. He wrote to his mother, still at Topaz, that he would be coming home soon. He got a letter back telling him that his father had been released from prison and had joined the family at the camp. Part of her letter read:

> You will need to have a long talk with your father, Yuki. He was so deeply shamed by being called a traitor. He has lost both his countries now, or at least he thinks so. But the army sent us a letter and told us that you received a medal for bravery. He will not say it, but he is pleased about that. For him, I feel sure, it saves the honor of our family. I am proud of you too, but for me the best thing is that you are alive and are coming home to us. I often feared that

would never happen. What I hope is that
you are feeling well. When you get here,
we need to make many decisions. We can
leave the camp now, if we choose, but we
do not know where we will go or what we
will do. You can help us make a plan.

What Yuki had wanted his mother to say was that she
would look after him for a time, that she would help him
think through his own future. But if his father was broken
by his experience, Yuki would have to help his mother
figure things out for the family. The problem was, he still
found himself unable to concentrate. He would have to
take one day at a time for now, and try to trust that he
would eventually become himself again.

He stayed at the hospital another three weeks, and
then, early in March, he received his discharge papers and
his train tickets. He sent a telegram to his parents that he
would soon be on his way but that he didn't know exactly
what day he would reach the camp. Then he boarded the
train and began the long cross-country ride. He rather
liked the monotony of it, liked watching the countryside,
and he liked letting the world come back to him a little at
a time. He didn't sleep well, but sleep was something he
had learned to fear anyway. He was still having dreams,
almost every night, and most of them put him back in the
battles he wanted to forget.

Yuki didn't say much to the travelers on the train, and no one seemed overly eager to talk to him. What he noticed, however, was that most people, though not exactly friendly, were at least polite. He thought maybe that had more to do with his uniform than anything else, and he did notice that some people, particularly other soldiers, looked at his service medals, especially his Silver Star. One man said, "I haven't seen many Silver Stars. You must be quite a soldier to earn that." Yuki decided to accept the compliment. He only said, "I did my best."

It took Yuki two days to reach Denver, and he learned there that he would have a few hours to wait for a train to Ogden, Utah. With time on his hands, he asked a man where he might be able to get a haircut. He knew how thin and weak he looked; he might as well not show up with scruffy hair.

He followed the man's directions and walked down a nearby street to a barbershop. It was a big place, with six occupied barber chairs and seven or eight men waiting their turn in straight-backed chairs lined up along the wall. Yuki caught the smell of hair tonic as he walked in and was reminded of the barbershop in Berkeley he had always gone to. He liked the memory.

He spotted an empty seat and took a couple of steps toward it, but just then the barber standing behind the first chair spoke up, loudly. "Sorry, soldier, but we don't cut Jap hair here. You need to turn around and walk back out that door."

Yuki stopped. He felt as though he had been shot in the chest all over again, even felt a kind of weakness come over him, as though he might sink to the floor. But he wasn't angry. He was humiliated. He didn't look at anyone, even though he knew that all the customers were staring at him.

Nothing had changed. It was obvious to Yuki that he would never be accepted. This man had only said what people had been telling him all his life.

So he didn't speak, didn't show contempt. He simply turned and stepped toward the door.

And then a loud voice reverberated through the room. "Wait just a minute, Sergeant."

It felt like a command, as though an officer had spoken, and Yuki's response was to spin around and stand at attention. But a bulky man was walking toward him—and he wasn't dressed in a uniform. The man was looking at the barber, not at Yuki.

"I think I misunderstood what you just said, mister. Because it sounded like you just told a decorated war hero that you wouldn't cut his hair."

Yuki glanced at the barber, who was standing straight, his scissors in one hand, a comb held high in the other.

"Do you recognize a Silver Star when you see one?"

The barber's hands dropped a little, but he didn't respond. He was a small man, bald headed.

"That *is* a Silver Star on the sergeant's chest, and it means he fought with *valor*, that he performed acts of bravery that went beyond the normal expectation for a soldier."

The barber gave a slight nod.

"Do you know a Purple Heart when you see one?"

Another little nod.

"I don't think you do. It means that while you were working here, being careful not to cut yourself with a pair of sharp scissors, this man was *shedding his blood* for his country. Now, tell me where you get the nerve to tell *him* that you won't cut his hair."

"It's just . . . something . . ."

The big man looked at Yuki. "Sergeant, I see by your shoulder patch that you were a member of the 442nd Regimental Combat Team." He stepped forward. "My name's Blaine Austin. I'm proud to meet you."

He held out his hand and Yuki shook it, as firmly as he could. "Thank you," he said. "My name's Yukus Naka-hara."

Mr. Austin looked back at the barber. "Do you know that for the size of their regiment, the Japanese soldiers who fought with this sergeant have received more decorations than any other unit in the American army? I fought alongside their troops in Italy, and I'll tell you, they are brave soldiers." He pointed a finger at the barber. "Now, listen to me. You cut this man's hair right now, and when

you're finished I want you to thank him for the honor."
He nodded to the man in the barber chair. "Why don't
you step down from that chair for a few minutes? Let the
sergeant sit down and get his hair cut first."

"Sure," the customer said, and he got up.

"Go ahead, Sergeant Nakahara. You take that chair.
But before you do, I want every man in this shop to stand
up and salute you."

It took a few seconds, but every man did stand—the
men who had been waiting and the ones with cloths
over them in the barber chairs. All of them saluted Yuki,
including the barbers, and they waited until Yuki returned
the salute. It was all he could do to hold back his tears.

The man who had given up his chair motioned for
him to sit down. But Yuki didn't want that to happen.
"No, that's all right. You finish your haircut. I'll wait my
turn. I'd like to get to know some of these fellows." He
looked around. "I get the feeling a lot of you have served
in the war." Most of the men were nodding.

"Stick around and talk to us then," Mr. Austin said.
"But get your hair cut first."

The barber nodded, so Yuki sat down in the barber
chair. The man who had been sitting there handed over
the cloth that had been covering him.

"It was my boss who told us not to cut your hair," the
barber said. "He thought other customers wouldn't like it.
But I'm not like that."

A few of the men chuckled, but Yuki didn't. He said, "I understand. You don't have to explain." He reached out and shook the barber's hand.

So Yuki got his hair cut, and the barber didn't charge him for it. And afterward, Yuki sat by Blaine Austin. They talked about the war in Italy, and then about the lost battalion in France. Everyone listened in. When Yuki left, he shook hands with everyone in the place, thanked them all. He wasn't naive enough to think he was finished with insults, but at least for the moment, in a barbershop in Denver, he felt like an American.

CHAPTER 18

Yuki took a train to Ogden and then a bus to Delta, Utah. He hadn't notified his family about his arrival because he hadn't known exactly when he would get there, and in any case, he wanted to walk in unannounced so that no one would make a fuss. When he arrived in Delta, he saw a Japanese man outside the little train station and asked how he could get a ride to Topaz. The man told him that a bus from the camp was in town and Yuki could catch that. He was an older man with heavy eyelids and a wrinkled neck. He spoke with a thick accent. "You home from war?" he asked.

"Yes, sir," Yuki said.

"You the Nakahara boy?"

"Yes."

"You great hero. Win many medals, I see." He pointed to Yuki's chest.

Yuki didn't say much, only thanked the man, but before he caught the bus, he took the Silver Star and the Purple Heart off his uniform. He didn't want anyone asking him to tell the story of how he had earned the medals.

When Yuki reached the camp and got off the bus, he felt the cold wind he remembered all too well. Spring had not come yet to this high altitude. The desert was white and lumpy, with a layer of recent snow over the greasewood and sagebrush. But he found the camp gate wide open, and when a soldier saw him in uniform, he stepped out from the guard's shed and said, "I see you're in the 442nd. Everyone in the States knows about you men. Here at the camp, your people all talk about you."

Yuki only nodded, but this was something new. Before he had left the camp, the guards had sometimes been polite, but they had rarely been friendly or respectful. And as Yuki walked through the rows of barracks, he saw other changes. He could see that the AJA residents had done more to fix up the place. They had planted more gardens and some had used rocks to mark the planted areas. But there were also fewer people. He knew why, of course: Many of those interned in the camp had been allowed to leave and had been moving to other cities around the country. Some, according to his mother's letters, had even been allowed to go back to the West Coast.

When Yuki reached his block of barracks, he saw a few people he knew, and they came to him, shook his hand.

All of them wanted to tell him the same thing: They had read about him. He was a hero. "Every soldier is a hero," Yuki told one man. But the man shook his head, told Yuki again the things he had read, and after that, Yuki didn't try to explain. He doubted that anyone would understand.

Yuki found his mother in the quarters where the family had lived before. He quietly opened the door and saw that she was alone. She was sitting at a table, mending a shirt, staring down at a little rip in the sleeve. Softly he said, "Hello, Mother."

She looked up and stared at him for a couple of seconds, as though she was trying to comprehend what she was seeing. "Oh, my," she said. She dropped her sewing and cupped her hands over her face. A little sob burst from her throat. But then she was up and coming to him. "We didn't expect you until tomorrow or the next day," she said.

"I know." He took her in his arms, thought she seemed thinner than before.

Yuki held his mother for a long time. He remembered how often he had longed for her to comfort him this way while he had been in Italy and France. When she finally stepped back to look at him, he saw that she had aged, looked worn down.

"Oh, Yuki," she said, "you look so old, so sad. What have they done to you?"

He didn't try to answer. But the emotions he had held

back so long finally spilled over. He had wept for Shig, but only privately. Now he took his mother in his arms once more and allowed himself to cry hard. He felt like a child again, when only Mother could give him solace after some little injury or disappointment. He clung tight to her as sobs came in powerful waves.

His mother held him, caressed his head, patted him. "It's okay. It's okay," she kept saying. "You made it back to us. You made it home."

"I didn't think I would. You'll never know how far away I've been, Mother. You'll never understand."

"I know how far away from us you *felt*, Yuki. I know how much I missed you."

The sobs came again, and now his mother was crying as hard as he was.

"It's all right," she kept telling him. "You're here. You're home now."

But this wasn't home. He wouldn't be home until he returned to California. "Why are you still here?" he finally managed to ask. "You said that people are leaving now."

"We'll talk about all that," Mother said. But she didn't let go of him yet. "Are you still hurt?" she asked. "You look so hurt."

"I'm getting better. I don't feel much pain now." He pulled back a little. He needed to sit down. He realized how exhausted he was, how much the long train and bus rides had cost him. He looked toward the chairs at the table.

"Sit down with me a few minutes," Mother said. "Before the others come back."

Yuki wiped the tears from his face, took some long breaths, and then pulled out a chair and sat at the table. His mother sat on the opposite side.

Yuki looked around the room. Things were about the same; he wasn't sure why they seemed different. Then he realized that the plywood that had been nailed over the bare studs of the walls was painted now, and Mother had hung some pictures. One was a photograph of him in his uniform, looking much younger. It was a gift he had sent from Camp Shelby before he had been shipped out.

"Where is everyone?" Yuki asked.

"They're all at school. They'll be home before long." She searched in an apron pocket for a handkerchief, and she wiped her tears away. Then she reached across the table and took hold of his hand. "Mick will graduate in a few months. But he works at the dining hall after school. He's been a big help to me, Yuki. He's grown up a lot."

"Where's Father?"

"He sits with the men. They play Go, or they talk—in Japanese." She leaned back a little and folded her arms. "Your father's not the same, Yuki. Don't expect him to be the man you remember."

"But I never knew him before. How will I know the

change?" Yuki had never said anything like that to his mother. He didn't know why he could be honest with her now.

"He doesn't let anyone know him, Yuki. He doesn't know how. But they took the life out of him by keeping him locked up so long. He liked to work hard, to grow his vegetables, to enjoy the harvest and collect the coins he could earn. That meant he was a man, that he was providing for his family. They took all that away."

"What will he do now? When are you planning to leave?"

"They're only letting a certain number go back to California. We can apply. But we have no land, Yuki. What would we do there now?"

"Can we rent land again? And maybe buy it, in time?"

"I don't know. The hatred is still there. The people don't want us back."

"Some people tell me they've read about our regiment. I've even had a few say to me that they appreciate what we did over there."

"Yes, I read it in the newspapers, and when they let us go into Delta, some of the white ladies are very nice to me now. But Yuki, we're still the enemy to most people. The hatred could get worse when our troops attack Japan. So many American boys will die. We might be facing the darkest days of all in the next year."

Yuki was accustomed to thinking of the war as

winding down. It was hard to accept the idea that years of fighting might still be ahead in the Pacific.

Mother reached for Yuki's hand again. "What happened to your face?" she asked.

"I got hit by some . . ." He didn't know what to call it, and he didn't want to tell the story. "Debris. I just got some little cuts. They're mostly healed now. I guess I'll have a few scars."

"Are you healing where they shot you?"

"I am. But I was lucky. The bullets missed my heart—one of them by just an inch or so. It went through my lung and it nicked an artery, but they operated on me and fixed those things. They tell me it will still take a while to rebuild my strength."

"But what about *you*? Are you all right?"

He tried to think of the answer. How could he describe the things he had experienced, all the stuff that was in his head? Yuki only said, "I'll be all right. The doctors weren't sure I would live at first, but I did. And I get a little stronger every day."

"What's happened inside you, Yuki? I see something in your eyes—some kind of sadness."

"I know what you mean. But I'm going to put everything behind me. That's what I have to do." He watched her face, saw her doubt. He knew he couldn't let her suffer that way. "Don't be too concerned. I'll get back to normal. Maybe I can take a train to California. I'll find us some land to rent. I'll wear my medals, and maybe some-one will like that—maybe give us a chance. We could start another farm. Father would have something to live for again. Maybe it's what I would like too."

What he knew was that he had invented every word of what he'd just said, never having thought about any of it before that moment. The truth was, he had no idea what he wanted to do, but he had to tell her something.

"I want you to go to college, Yuki. You can do that. The government will pay your tuition now that you've been a soldier."

"Yeah, I might like that. The main thing is, we'll figure things out."

Yuki tried to look happy, but he wasn't sure he was doing very well. Still, his mother liked his words. She was nodding, saying, "Yes, yes. That's what I keep telling your father. Yukus is coming home. He'll help us make a plan."

"Should I go find him now?"

"No. Not with the other men there. He won't know what to do or what to say in front of them. Just sit here with me for now. I need to hear more about you."

So Yuki stayed, and he talked. He told her a little about the training in Mississippi, about the places he had seen in Italy and France, about crossing the ocean, once by sea, once by air. But he didn't mention Shig, and she didn't ask. And he said not a word about the battles he had fought, didn't tell her about Mat or any of the other friends he had lost.

He changed the subject when he could, asked about May. "She's all right," Mother said. "We have two rooms now, instead of just this one. That gives her and Kay more privacy. They needed that."

"They're almost grown up, I guess," Yuki said. "It's hard for me to think of them that way."

"May is definitely growing up. What worries me is that she likes boys too much, and she's too pretty for her own good. She's also too American to ever accept the old ways. She tells your father exactly what she thinks. When he first came here, he tried to control her, but he's already given up on that."

"Is she going to be okay?"

"She's going to be an American woman—with opinions and a career. She may like boys, but she claims she won't marry for a long time. She wants to go to college, and she says she's going to be a doctor. She'll probably do it too. She's smarter than any of us, and she goes after the things she wants without the slightest self-doubt."

"That's good. Women are going to do more things now. I just hope a medical school will accept her."

"That's what I worry about—that America won't let her be who she is. You used to tell us that our boys would join the army and change people's minds. But I don't know. Will it ever happen?"

"Maybe." And then he told her about the barbershop in Denver, and the men saluting him.

Tears came to her eyes again as she listened to the story. "That is reason for hope, Yuki. It's hard to see any change while we're still here behind this barbed wire. Maybe when we get back with the people, at least some of them will see us differently."

Yuki was not as confident about that as he wanted to be. At the very least, he knew it would take time.

"So what about Kay? How's she doing?"

"She'll be crazy to see you. All she does is brag about you. All the kids do. They'll want to know everything about the war." But when Yuki glanced away, she added, "But you won't tell them. I can see that already."

"No, I won't."

"Tell them enough so that they won't think it's wonderful, the way they do now. Especially Mick. He talks about killing 'Krauts.' He says he wants the war to last a long time so he can get there. He's almost old enough now, and I know what he thinks: that he can be a hero like his brother."

"We can't let him go when he turns eighteen, Mother. I don't want him to go at all."

"He'll be drafted, Yuki. It's not like it was when you *decided* to join the army. I didn't want you to go, and you went all the same. But there's no changing that—the way boys all want to prove that they're men."

Yuki tried to think of himself back when he had enlisted, what he had said and felt. Those memories were still in his head, and yet they seemed part of some other person—a boy he no longer knew.

After a time, Father came home. He stepped through the door and then stopped. "Yukus," he said, and his tone expressed his surprise. But he didn't come to Yuki, didn't greet him. He only stood in the doorway and stared.

"Father. It's so good to see you." Yuki got up, walked around the table, and stepped close. He had told himself he would embrace his father when he saw him, but he couldn't bring himself to do it, and Father actually stepped back a little, as though he feared that Yuki would try.

"We are very happy you have come back," Father said. It was more English than he usually used. Yuki thought maybe he had improved his English while he was in prison.

"It's good to be back, Father."

There was a long silence after that, and neither could look the other in the eye. Finally, Father said, "Are you getting better?"

"Yes. I'm improving pretty fast now."

"Very good."

"I was just telling Mother, I'll take a trip to California and see whether I can rent some land. I'm a veteran now, and that ought to count for something. I could rent a farm in my name, but it would really be your place. We could farm again, just like before."

"The war is not over, Yukus. Not for me. They call me traitor."

"That's changing, Father. People will get over that. And if my name is on the paperwork, it won't matter anyway."

"It matters to me."

"I understand. I'm just saying, we can get started again, and eventually people will forget all the hatred and . . . you know, we know how to get along with people." But Yuki wasn't convincing himself, and he knew he wasn't convincing his father.

Father stood straight for a time, seeming to consider, and then he said, "Yukus, you do not like to be Japanese. You never want that."

Yuki nodded. "I know what you mean, Father. I didn't want to be Japanese when I was a kid. But I've learned some things since then. You taught me honor. That's what helped us Japanese boys fight so well. I'm not ashamed to be Japanese now. I'm proud of it."

Father nodded.

"But I'm also an American. I'm proud of that, too."

Father nodded again. Yuki thought it was as big a sign of satisfaction as he could ever expect. But then his father reached out and the two shook hands. At this, Yuki broke through the silent resistance he had known all his life. He wrapped his arms around his father and held him tight. His father didn't clasp him back, didn't say anything, but at least he let it happen.

CHAPTER 19

Yuki's sisters came home to the barracks not long after that, and then Mick came in too. It all seemed strange—the family together, with everything to talk about but nowhere to start. But his sisters hugged him over and over, and they told him he looked good, even though he knew he didn't. And everyone smiled and looked around at one other, words clearly not the best way to communicate what they were all feeling.

Mick did ask a few questions about the war, but Yuki purposely kept his answers vague, and everyone seemed to realize that he wasn't going to offer any details. May admitted, "Sometimes I thought we'd never see you again. So many died, Yuki. We heard about our boys dying all the time."

Yuki knew what she meant. The local newspaper carried pictures of all the Utah soldiers who had died or been wounded. But May meant "our" boys—the Japanese American boys who had joined the Four-Four-Two. She also meant Shig, of course, but he wasn't ready to start that conversation.

Yuki gripped May's hand. "I was almost sure I would never see you again," he said. He looked around. "Or any of you." The room fell silent, and soon tears were in everyone's eyes. Yuki reached his other hand out to Kay. She was a skinny little thing, but cute, and he was glad she hadn't changed too much.

After a time the family walked together to the dining hall, and even though there were not so many people lined up for dinner as there once had been, Yuki created a bit of a sensation. An article in the *Topaz Times* had reported that Yuki had received a Silver Star. The description of his heroic acts had been quoted from the citation that had been included with his medal, so everyone had read that he'd faced enemy fire and put his own life on the line to save the men of his platoon.

People kept coming, everyone wanting to shake his hand, tell him how glad they were he had survived his wounds and how proud they were of him. But some of the people had lost their sons, and he hardly knew what to say to them.

All the while, Yuki knew that he needed to see Shig's family. Mother had told him that the Omuras hadn't moved away yet. He wasn't sure he was up to talking to them, but he also knew it would be obvious he was avoiding them if he didn't go by right away.

So after he ate his dinner, Yuki walked to the barracks where the Omuras lived. He found no one there and assumed they had gone to their own dining hall in their block of barracks. He waited for them to return, and while he waited, he became increasingly nervous. He was standing outside the barracks, shivering in the late-afternoon cold, when he saw Shig's parents, with Keiko, walking toward him. Mr. Omura was a small man, so much like Shig in his appearance that it was startling—and painful for Yuki to look at him.

Yuki took a better look at Keiko and realized that he hardly knew her. He had known that she was eighteen now, but in his mind she had remained the innocent kid he had liked to dance with. She was still pretty, but she had taken on a graceful way of walking that he never would have expected. And her round face had become more sculpted, more womanly.

Yuki stood before the three of them, bowed his head a little. Mr. Omura responded to his bow, stopped and lowered his head for a moment. "Yukus, we heard you were back. It is wonderful to see you," he said.

Yuki took a breath. He had wondered whether the Omuras hated him, whether they blamed him. He had prepared himself to accept their anger quietly if they refused to talk to him. Mrs. Omura walked close, took

Yuki's hand in hers. "It's so good to see you," she said. Yuki had written one letter to the Omuras while he was still in the hospital in France, and he had told them, in general terms, that Shig had died valiantly, but he had not heard anything back from them.

Keiko was staying close to her father. Yuki could see that her face was flushed. She clearly didn't know what to do. Yuki didn't know either. "It's nice to see you, Keiko," he finally said. "You look . . . very nice."

He saw her color deepen. She was wearing a pale blue dress with a white collar. She seemed rather dressed up for a weeknight, and he wondered, had she heard from someone that he had arrived? Had she put on her favorite dress for him? Had she been looking forward to this moment, or did she have lots of boyfriends now?

But there were other matters he had to deal with before he worried about that. "I have some things I need to say to all of you," Yuki said.

Mrs. Omura touched his arm. "Come in. Sit down with us."

So they walked inside to a room the same size and shape as the one the Nakaharas lived in. Mrs. Omura had done even more to fix theirs up. There were cloth coverings on the walls—cream-colored sheets—and there were prints of mountains and lakes. A little lampshade covered the lightbulb that hung in the middle of the room. It seemed a feeble attempt to make such a place a home, but

Yuki admired Mrs. Omura's neatness, her obvious desire to make the best of things.

Yuki sat down with the Omuras on wooden chairs that Mr. Omura set out in a kind of rectangle. "You were badly wounded, I believe," Mr. Omura said. "You didn't say much about that in your letter, but I think it was worse than you admitted."

"By the time I wrote to you, it wasn't so bad," Yuki said. "I was shot here." He touched his chest. He thought of saying that he had been lucky to survive, but that would only raise the question of why Shig had not been as fortunate. "I'm doing quite well now. I know I look awful, but I'll get my strength back."

"I'm sure you will," Mr. Omura said.

And Mrs. Omura said, "You look fine, Yukus. Don't worry about that."

Yuki glanced at Keiko, saw that she was looking back at him. He wondered what she was thinking. Was she shy to be around him now, or was she hoping he wouldn't pay attention to her?

Yuki took a breath. With his eyes directed straight ahead, not at any faces, he said, "Mr. and Mrs. Omura, I was the one who convinced Shigeo that he should join the army. I wish now I had never done that. I want you to know how very sorry I am. I wish he had never listened to me."

"No, Yukus," Mr. Omura said. "This is not right." He

waited for Yuki to look at him. "Shigeo brought great honor to our family. It's what you said in your letter, and it's what your platoon leader said in the letter he sent us. We are very proud of our son."

"It wasn't you, Yuki," Mrs. Omura said. "He made up his own mind. He talked with us over and over about his decision. When he decided, he told us he would never feel good about himself if he stayed home while others went away to defend our country."

"But I'm the one who kept saying that to him."

"That doesn't matter. It's what he felt too. And he wrote letters to us, saying that he was proud to wear the uniform of his nation. He told us he was proud to be part of such a fine group of soldiers."

Yuki felt forgiven—more than he thought he deserved. He didn't want to shame himself in front of Keiko, but he couldn't hold back his tears. He leaned forward, his elbows on his knees, and fought to control himself. When he could find his voice, he said, "We were brothers, Shig and I. We got each other through so many battles, and we always came out all right. And then we were both shot on the same hill." He fought his emotions hard again, and then he said what he had never said out loud. "I don't understand why he died and I lived. The world would be a better place if it had been the other way around."

"No, Yuki." Mrs. Omura got up and stepped toward Yuki. She placed her hand carefully on his shoulder, and then she put her fingers under his chin and lifted it. "You must never say this again, never think it. These are things we do not understand. God decides, and in our family, we trust God. Shigeo was a noble boy, and he will be precious in our hearts forever, but we have no regrets about his service. He sacrificed his life for the good of our world."

Yuki drew in a breath. He finally felt some relief after all these weeks of worry and remorse. "Thank you," he whispered.

"Can you tell us anything more about his death?"

Yuki nodded. "Yes."

Mrs. Omura walked back to her chair and sat down.

Yuki tried to think what to say to them. He didn't want to put all that blood in their minds. "Shig was small, of course," he said, "and some of our trainers didn't think he would make much of a soldier. But he became a courageous fighter. I want you to know, we were both wounded trying to save Americans who were trapped behind enemy lines."

"Yes. This is what we have been told," Mr. Omura said.

"But what Shig did was especially brave. I was in a bad spot, but he came to help me. When the bullets knocked him down, I tried to keep him alive, but he was hurt too bad. His heart kept beating for about a minute, but he wasn't conscious. He didn't have to suffer."

The picture of it all—Shig on the ground, the open

wound in his abdomen—came forcefully back to Yuki's mind. But he described none of that.

Tears were dripping from Yuki's chin again.

"This is war," Mr. Omura said. But tears were in his eyes too, and that was something Yuki had never expected from him.

Yuki glanced at Keiko and saw that she was also crying. She met Yuki's eyes for just a moment, and then she whispered, "You did what you could, so don't blame yourself. It's good that one of you could come back to us."

The words were huge to Yuki. He had worried for weeks that she would hold him responsible, would not want to see him.

"Life is full of pain," Mr. Omura said, "and I was raised to accept pain, not pity myself. We must be thankful that Shigeo is beyond suffering now."

Yuki nodded. But that seemed enough talk about pain; he wanted to say something that might leave them with better memories of Shig. He related some of the experiences he and Shig had shared. He told them of Shig running up the wall at Camp Shelby, showing the others how to make it over the top. He described the buddha-heads and the fun they liked to have, even told them about Muki Shimuzu offering to fight them on their first day in Mississippi—although he didn't tell them that Muki had been shot through the hip and carried off the battle-field, and would probably suffer difficulty with that all his life. Instead, he said a few things about digging foxholes together, looking out for one another. He described the day he and Shig had been blasted in the face and then sat in an alley and talked about their chances of getting home. But that was a little too tender for everyone, and Yuki decided he had said enough.

An hour had gone by, and everyone seemed satisfied with the conversation. Yuki finally thanked Mr. and Mrs. Omura for their goodness to him, and said, "We'll talk again. I have other stories, if you want to hear them."

"Yes. We would like that," Mr. Omura said. He shook Yuki's hand.

Yuki was stepping toward the door when Keiko touched his arm. "Yuki, do you remember the soda fountain I told you about in one of my letters?" she asked him.

"I do." And then he took a chance. "I read your letters many times, Keiko. They meant a great deal to me."

She blushed, looked down. "I'm glad to know it." She hesitated, and then said, "Would you like to see the soda fountain? I can show you."

This was what an American girl would say to a boy, and both her parents glanced down, clearly embarrassed. But Yuki liked the way Keiko was smiling. It was as though she were saying to him, "Would you like to be yourself again?"

The answer he gave her—and himself—surprised him. "Yes, I'd like that. Maybe I could come by sometime and—"

"We could walk over now. It's still early."

Yuki nodded. "Okay. That sounds swell. Thank you." He glanced at the Omuras. They looked pleased, and that relieved him. So he opened the door for Keiko, and she glanced at him as she walked out. He saw what seemed to be a glimmer of satisfaction and enough spark to suggest flirtation.

When they reached the little soda fountain, it didn't look like much from the outside, but it was the real thing inside. There were young people at the counter and the tables, and some were dancing in a little space at the far end of the room. The jukebox in the corner was playing a jive tune, rather loudly. It was as though his years in California, forgotten for such a long time, had suddenly dropped out of the sky and landed in Utah. "Let's dance," Keiko said.

Yuki hadn't thought of doing such a thing. He wasn't sure that he still knew the steps. But he smiled. "Okay," he said. "Help me remember."

It was surprising how it all came back, not just the steps, but the feel of it, even his energy. His body, his soul, hadn't felt this animated since he had left Topaz almost two years earlier. And Keiko was like a glint of life itself, wonderful to look at. Her dimples were flashing now, and she was both that sixteen-year-old girl he remembered and this new young woman he had just met.

They danced a couple of dances, they ate some ice

cream, and after a time they walked outside into the cool air.

"Are you really okay, Yuki?" Keiko asked. "From Shig's letters—and yours—I could tell that everything was really hard, even if you wouldn't come right out and say it."

Yuki didn't know how to tell her, didn't want to tell her, but he admitted, "It was worse than I . . . expected." Then he looked into her eyes. "Keiko, war should not exist. It's the worst thing human beings have thought up. It made me feel . . . dirty . . . to be part of it. Shig felt the same way."

"You and Shig were brave, though. You—"

"We were scared. Every minute."

"But you didn't let that stop you. You're a hero now."

"Keiko, we did our best. We all did. But it's not like the newspapers make it sound, or the movies, or . . ." Yuki stopped, and he made a decision. That was all he was going to say. No one could understand—except those who had been there.

He and Keiko walked out toward the barbed-wire fence. Keiko told him that the guards didn't worry anymore whether anyone approached it. What Yuki liked was being far enough away from the tar paper barracks to feel the grand space out under the sky. He knew the cold would soon force them back to their barracks, but for now, he wanted to be alone with Keiko, wanted to feel himself part of the universe. The first stars were coming out, sharper here in the desert than they had been in Europe. The beauty of that sky, the fading mountains off to the south, even the cold breeze seemed to say that God hadn't given up on the earth, no matter what humans chose to do to one another.

"What are you going to do now, Yuki?" Keiko asked.

"I don't know. Maybe go back to California."

"We feel the same way. We want to go back to Berkeley, or somewhere around there. And I want to go to college."

"You're really smart, aren't you?"

She laughed. "I don't know. I just know I'd like to be a teacher, but no one will hire me to teach in regular schools, so I don't know what to study."

"Be a teacher if that's what you want. Don't let anyone stop you."

"That's easy to say, but I'm not in control. I can only do what America will let me do."

"Things are going to change, Keiko."

"How? White people still don't accept us. What will change that?"

Yuki liked to think that the valor of the *Nisei* soldiers would make a difference in the way the nation thought about Japanese Americans—but he wasn't sure that it would. He tried to think why he still trusted that change was coming. He was quiet for a long time before he said,

"All my life I've wanted to be like everyone else—and pretend I'm not really Japanese. But that doesn't work. There was no better regiment in the army than the Four-Four-Two. But it wasn't that way in *spite* of our Japanese heritage. It was that way *because* of it. I think you should just go forward and be who you are. Once people really know you, they won't want to stand in your way."

Yuki was surprised by his own words. They were part of an idea that had been forming in his mind, but it wasn't something he had felt with such confidence before. He was pretty sure Keiko's future—and his—would be more difficult than he was admitting to her. But he was right all the same; he was sure of it.

"I don't know, Yuki. I don't think many people *want* to know us. It's easier to hate us—in a lump—than it is to get to know us one at a time."

"I know. But we're all like that. I've seen it in myself—you know, in the war. I wanted to hate all Germans, but every now and then I'd find out they were just regular people. After one of our battles, I found a German boy on the ground. He was dead, but he was curled up on his side, like a little kid in bed. All I could think was that he didn't want to be in this war any more than I did. It was probably the same for most of the Germans."

"But then, how could you . . ."

"Kill them?"

"Yes."

She was looking into his eyes, as though she wanted to understand what he had been through, but Yuki knew he could never tell her everything. He didn't want her to know that he was the one who had killed that German boy. He would think about that all his life, but he didn't want her to bear that burden with him.

"I'll tell you the truth. We mostly fought for each other—our Japanese brothers. But our *Nisei* regiment also lost a whole lot of men trying to save the lives of white guys we didn't even know. A lot of our men, including Shig, sacrificed their lives for those guys. By then we knew that they were our brothers too."

"I'm proud of Shig that he did that."

"You should be. In battle, you see it all the time: One guy lays down his own life to save the life of another. That's the one thing from war I want to remember. It gives me hope."

"But someone always thinks up another war. I don't know if the world will ever have peace for very long."

Yuki thought of the word "peace." It had always meant "no war" to him, but now it meant something he longed for more than anything else: comfort within himself, trust that the world was a good place and that he had a rightful role to play in it. "I want to believe that everyone's better impulses will win out sooner or later," he told Keiko.

Keiko smiled up at him. "Well . . . you give me hope,

and I haven't felt too much of that while I've been locked up in this camp."

Her words amazed Yuki. He had spent so many months feeling hopeless that he had never expected to find hope for himself, let alone offer hope to anyone else. He took a long breath and felt something let go. He had been tense for such a long time that he had forgotten how it felt to let himself . . . breathe. Just breathe.

Shig had died and Yuki had lived. Yuki knew that would always hurt, but he also knew he had to do the best he could with the life he had been granted—not just for himself, but for all the friends he had lost.

Keiko was as bright and beautiful as anyone he knew, and she was very close. He wanted more than anything to kiss her. It seemed a little too soon, too forward, to do that just yet . . . but he had felt dead these last few months, and now her eyes seemed to be saying, "Come back to life, Yuki. It's all right to do that."

He took another long, deep breath, and he felt a kind of lightness fill his chest. He had the feeling he was becoming himself again.

AUTHOR'S NOTE

The accomplishments of the 100th/442nd Regi-
mental Combat Team were widely known by the end of
World War II. But today, most people have no idea that
an all-*Nisei* military unit ever existed, or that its soldiers
fought so valiantly. Kathryn Shenkle, from the Center of
Military History, United States Department of Defense,
described the actions of the *Nisei* soldiers in a single sen-
tence: The "100th Infantry Battalion, and the "Go For
Broke" 442nd Regimental Combat Team is still the most
decorated unit in U.S. military history."[3]

---

3 Shenkle, Kathryn (May 2006). *"Patriots under Fire: Japanese
Americans in World War II"*. United States Department of Defense,
Department of the Army, Center of Military History. Archived from
the original on 23 June 2013.

The Go For Broke National Education Center published a document that provides a numerical depiction of what "most decorated" means in this case:

Japanese American WWII Soldiers—
Awards, Honors, and Statistics[4]

Note: The accurate numbers of individual awards, honors, and personnel counts are disputed. Statistics vary depending on the source, and many of these statistics are still being updated as new information comes to light. This list features the most accurate statistics that we could find, based on substantial research and comparison between existing sources.

Note: The awards listed do not include those given by foreign governments.

MEDALS AND HONORS AWARDED TO THE
100TH/442ND REGIMENTAL COMBAT TEAM

Number of men served:	about 18,000
Presidential Unit Citations:	7
Medals of Honor:	21
Distinguished Service Crosses:	29

---

4   Courtesy of Go For Broke National Education Center.

Silver Stars:	560,
	plus 28 Oak Leaf Clusters in lieu of second Silver Stars
Bronze Stars:	4,000,
	plus 1,200 Oak Leaf Clusters in lieu of second Bronze Stars
Legion of Merit Medals:	22
Soldier's Medals:	15
Purple Hearts:	9,486
Meritorious Service Unit Plaques:	2
Army Commendation Medals:	36
Division Commendations:	87
Distinguished Service Medals:	1
Combat Casualty Rate:	314%

While all these figures are impressive, some deserve special attention. The total number of soldiers—including replacements over the entire length of the war—was about 18,000, and a total of 9,486 Purple Heart medals were awarded. A Purple Heart is presented to a soldier who is wounded or injured in battle. Some men were wounded but returned to battle, and then received a second or third Purple Heart. Even with those multiple awards taken into account, approximately half of *all* soldiers in the 100th/442nd received wounds.

The most telling statistic is the combat casualty rate

of 314 percent. This means that the total number of soldiers in the regiment had to be replaced more than twice. For example, a platoon that started with approximately thirty men would have seen all thirty wounded or killed in action, then replaced, and this new platoon of men would also fall and have to be replaced. Some men made it all the way through the war, of course, but the majority did not survive unscathed. Eight hundred *Nisei* were killed in action, and most of those were members of the 100th/442nd. In addition, many suffered throughout their lives from serious wounds, and virtually all of them paid an emotional and mental price for having fought in some of the most difficult battles of the war.

Members of the 100th/442nd Regimental Combat Team march into battle on a muddy French road near the Vosges Forest.

As was the case with my fictional character, Yuki Nakahara, many of the men who fought with the Four-Four-Two set out to prove their loyalty. Their actions certainly received praise, and some Americans did change their minds about Japanese Americans being "the enemy." Still, the Japanese American soldiers who returned from the war, along with the thousands of families who were finally released from internment camps, were often subject to racist insults. While the character and personalities of Japanese people vary as much as in any group or culture, of course, the heritage that these abused people shared prepared them to respond to mistreatment with grace and restraint. They were excellent contributors to their communities, and gradually, other Americans respected them for that. Young people today may have difficulty imagining that Japanese Americans were ever the subject of such prejudice and cruelty.

Germany surrendered to the Allies on May 8, 1945, and then, with the dropping of two atomic bombs on Japan in August of that year, the war in the Pacific also ended. On July 15, 1946, President Harry S. Truman met with the men of the Four-Four-Two on the Ellipse south of the White House. He reviewed the troops and presented them with a Presidential Citation—a recognition given to military units that distinguish themselves in battle. It was the seventh citation honoring their valor and effectiveness. These were President Truman's words of commendation:

It is a very great pleasure to me today to be able to put the seventh regimental citation on your banners.

You are to be congratulated on what you have done for this great country of ours. I think it was my predecessor who said that Americanism is not a matter of race or creed, it is a matter of the heart.

You fought for the free nations of the world along with the rest of us. I congratulate you on that, and I can't tell you how very much I appreciate the privilege of being able to show you just how much the United States of America thinks of what you have done.

You are now on your way home. *You fought not only the enemy, but you fought prejudice—and you have won.* Keep up that fight, and we will continue to win—to make this great Republic stand for just what the Constitution says it stands for: the welfare of all the people all the time.[5]
[Italics added]

---

5   Harry S. Truman, "Remarks upon Presenting a Citation to a Nisei Regiment," July 15, 1946. The American Presidency Project website, http://www.presidency.ucsb.edu/index.php.

President Harry S. Truman reviews the 100th/442nd Regimental Combat Team after presenting them with a Presidential Citation, July 15, 1946.

It was perhaps premature for President Truman to announce that the victory over prejudice had been won, but change had begun in the hearts and minds of the American people and has continued to our day.

This history of racial prejudice during World War II should cause us to ponder our own time. We should ask ourselves: Are there people or groups of other national origins, races, religions, sexual orientations, or other arbitrary classifications whom I disrespect or misjudge? Those who hated Japanese Americans during World War II probably wonder at themselves now and regret the way they once behaved. It's good for us to consider what attitudes toward groups or individuals we will someday regret. Better yet, couldn't we discover and acknowledge our current prejudices and put them aside now?

I appreciate the assistance I received from the Go For Broke National Education Center. This organization and museum serves as an excellent starting place for anyone seeking to do further research on this subject. I'm also indebted to Jane Beckwith, president of the board of the Topaz Museum and Education Center in Delta, Utah. She has guided my research on the Central Utah Relocation Center for many years.

My wife, Kathy, read and reread this manuscript as she has all of my manuscripts during a whole lifetime of writing. She's kind enough to make me feel good about the stories I write and, fortunately, tough enough to point out the weaknesses. She, along with my editor, Emma Ledbetter, helped me make extensive revisions to *Four-Four-Two* when I was hoping that I was almost finished. Thanks to the two of them, the novel is much stronger than it would have been. What a joy it is to share the process of researching and writing with such supportive, good people.